A DARLING BAY CHRISTMAS

THREE HEARTWARMING SHORT STORIES

RACHAEL HERRON   JULIET BLACKWELL
SOPHIE LITTLEFIELD

HGA PUBLISHING

CONTENTS

COPYRIGHT

*L*ast fall, Sophie, Juliet, and Rachael went to the coast to have a girls' writing weekend. We did a 1000-piece jigsaw. We drank too much wine and ate lots of fancy cheese. We floated in the hot tub and looked up at the stars. We walked a massive dog named Nugget (Juliet's) and a tiny dog named Dozy (Rachael's). We laughed and cried together, as we always do. Someone may have put one of the others into an online dating app and immediately (and accidentally!) propositioned her son's favorite teacher. (Oops.)

And at some point, we had the idea to write a series of linked short holiday stories, all set in Rachael's world of Darling Bay.

See, we all know Darling Bay, even though it's not exactly real. North of San Francisco, Darling Bay has the flavors of Bolinas and Bodega Bay and Gualala and Big Sur, all mashed up together. It's a small village on the rugged northern coast, populated by people who fall in love often and well.

Even though white Christmases are rare, they can happen in Darling Bay.

Love, which isn't rare there, happens a lot, especially when mistletoe and carols hang in the cool, foggy air.

Please enjoy.

love,

Juliet, Sophie, and Rachael

ADDISON'S PAST

ADDISON'S PAST

BY JULIET BLACKWELL

Addison couldn't remember the last time she'd received an actual handwritten letter in the mail.

It *was* almost Christmas, though, and among her circle of acquaintances were a few stalwarts who still sent holiday cards sheathed in bright red and green envelopes and sealed with stickers in the shape of wreathes and snowmen wearing scarves and top hats. Now and then Addison also received scribbled postcards from the loyal friends who had stuck with her all last year through what she liked to think of as "the year she found herself." Others of her acquaintance—not without cause, she admitted—called last year "Addison's year of selfishness."

But this wasn't a Christmas card or a postcard—it was a genuine old-fashioned letter, a plain white business-size envelope with Addison's name and address printed on the front in a spidery, shaky hand. In the left-hand corner was the sender's name and address: Earl Pickett, 25 Abalone Lane, Darling Bay, California.

Addison shifted her heavy bag higher on her right

shoulder, gripping her briefcase—crammed with work to do tonight—tightly in her left hand as she shut and locked her mailbox in the lobby of the pre-war New York City building where she'd been subletting an apartment for the past year. The owner was returning soon, so Addison needed to move. But figuring that out would have to wait until she decided whether to accept the job offer in San Francisco, and she couldn't decide *that* until her current New York employer made a counter-offer. Oh, how she prayed the firm would make a counter-offer.

As much as she loved San Francisco, it was *way* too close to Darling Bay.

The apartment building's small elevator pinged its arrival, and she stepped in, pushed the button for her floor, ripped open the white envelope, and started to read.

And just like that, her well-thought-out, meticulously-crafted holiday-avoidance plans fell apart.

This would be her first holiday season apart from Dylan in four years, and Addison had been determined to create a new tradition. For the first time in her life, she would spend the holidays somewhere besides Darling Bay. *Anywhere* besides Darling Bay. Six months ago she had closed her eyes and stuck a pin into a map of the Caribbean. On the fourth try the pin landed in the Turks and Caicos. The name appealed to her, so she booked a resort vacation for one at a four-star hotel, went on a diet, and started shopping for bikinis. She intended to take a lot of photos with various handsome, scantily-dressed men and post them to social media, even though she never did that sort of thing, just so that anyone and everyone who saw them would know she was having the time of her life.

Addison died a little inside, just thinking about it.

Still, it was better than going home to Darling Bay, where memories lurked around every corner: the time Addie had first brought Dylan to the Golden Spike saloon where bar regular Norma had tricked him into buying her six drinks in a row. The time the aunties insisted on reading their tarot cards, Dylan sitting barefoot and cross-legged on the worn Turkish carpet, surrounded by candles, gamely feigning interest and cracking jokes, sneaking Addie secret glances, winning over the hearts of all four aunties. The magical little rental cottage behind Earl Pickett's place, called Siren Song, which was a converted water tower. The main floor was the living room with a tiny kitchen and a small bathroom, complete with a claw-footed tub. A ladder near the bathroom led up to the loft, a large space that held nothing but a huge bed covered with the softest cream-colored comforter in the world, and topped by a patchwork quilt. The aunties had made the quilt for Earl Pickett decades ago, when he returned from the Korean War.

Or...the time she drank way too much tequila and decided Dylan was flirting with her old high school nemesis, Vivian Engel, who was looking cute-as-a-button in a Santa's Elf costume, and Addison had started dirty dancing with a firefighter named Smoke (who was gay, but Dylan hadn't known that) and Dylan went ballistic and wound up starting a barroom brawl, during which he broke the bar back mirror, not to mention his arm.

That was when Dylan, made clumsy by his new cast, had packed his bag and stormed out of the Siren Song into a chilly, misty night.

Christmas Eve of last year.

The elevator pinged, and the door slid open. Addison hurried down the hall and managed to get her key in the door of her apartment, dumped her bags on the kitchen counter, then re-read the letter:

Dear Addie,

If you're reading this, it means I've moved on to the great beyond. Don't be sad—I'm not. I've had a good run, and I'm ready.

Anyway, on to more important issues. Such as your plans for Christmas.

You didn't make reservations this year, but of course I always keep Siren Song open for you over the holidays. I know your last trip here didn't go so well –everyone's still talking about it!—but I hope you'll come back to Darling Bay for my memorial service. There will be a Very Important Announcement: the identity of the new Darling Bay Santa Claus! Wouldn't want to miss that.

And just in case you were wondering: Dylan's band is playing in Cabo San Lucas over the holidays, so you don't have to worry.

I'll see you on the other side, my dear.

Love always, Earl

He had enclosed a little charm, which Addison recognized as one of her Aunt Maisie's talismans.

Addison stroked the beaded leather talisman as she collapsed into a chair, blowing out a long breath. When Aunt Willa called to tell her of Earl's passing last week, Addison had been saddened by the news but had not planned on flying cross-country to attend the memorial service. She needed to spend the holidays by herself, becoming accustomed to her new, non-Dylan normal, starting with a solo adventure to the Caribbean.

Earl's letter changed all that. She couldn't very well refuse to attend a memorial when she had been personally invited by the guest of honor. Earl deserved better.

And as long as Dylan wasn't there, she could get through a few days in Darling Bay. She could make it through Christmas Sunday. She would do it for Earl.

Dylan. Her stomach clenched. As usual when she thought of him, his face appeared in front of her: the five o'clock shadow, the strong chin, the little crinkles that had just started to develop at the corners of his dark, romantic eyes. They tilted downward at the edges, ever so slightly, giving him a whisper of vulnerability…

Forget him, Addie, she told herself for the thousandth time in the last twelve months. *You made your choice, and it was the right one.* They wanted different things out of life. Dylan had been very clear: he wanted marriage, a home, a family, *children.* After years of touring with his band, he wanted to put down roots, to belong somewhere. Dylan would have been perfectly happy to settle in Darling Bay. Forever.

But Addison had left Darling Bay at the age of seventeen to go to college in Chicago, running as far as she could from her hometown—and more importantly, from repeating the mistakes her mother had made. It had been just the two of them, ever since Addison's father abandoned them. Stephanie did all the things mothers were supposed to do: she baked cupcakes for school birthday parties, never missed a Back To School Night or school play, attended Parent-Teacher Association meetings, packed nutritious lunches, ensured Addison did her homework and did it well.

But her mother hated every minute of it, and Addison suffered because of it, only too aware that she was a major cause of her mother's unhappiness. And her father's unexplained abandonment was always there, lurking just beneath the surface of their interactions. Stephanie often warned Addison: *Having children changes everything. You just watch. You lose your whole life, your sense of self.*

Their relationship improved when Addison got older and more independent, but the hurt she felt at her mother's rejection and her father's unexplained abandonment was always there, lurking just beneath the surface of their interactions. Still, Addison loved her mother, and when Stephanie got sick a few years back, Addison had decided to go to law school in San Francisco to be closer to her. So really, it was *Stephanie's* fault that Addison had met Dylan.

After graduating at the top of her class, Addison had been spending all day every day studying for the notoriously difficult bar exam. One evening she had packed up her computer and sheaf of notes and went to study at a pub on Mission Street because if she had to spend one more minute in her tiny apartment she was going to hurt somebody. The moment she walked in she spotted Dylan: leaning against the bar, wearing a dark leather jacket, he projected confidence and a bad attitude...but then there were those eyes.

Dylan had become her good-time bad-boy. He was her reward for the long days and sleepless nights spent studying for the bar exam that would make her a full-fledged lawyer. The hours of work had paid off professionally: Addison passed the bar on her first try and was offered a junior associate position at a top-flight law firm in New York City, just as she had always dreamed.

But as devoted as she was to her career, Addison wanted more. "All work and no play makes Addison a dull girl," she would chant to herself as, every six weeks or so, she hopped on a plane to meet Dylan wherever his band was playing: New Orleans or St. Louis or Chicago or even Boise. For a few precious days Addison wasn't a hard-nosed, hard-driving attorney who spent her days prepping cases, reading piles of mind-numbing depositions and endless court decisions searching for precedents, and plotting arcane legal strategies. She was the guitar player's girlfriend. She would watch from the wings as Dylan played, his long fingers on the struts, his hips thrust just so, radiating a masculine intensity...and after the gig they would return to the hotel in the wee small hours and make love the rest of the night. If they made it as far as the hotel room.

And once a year, at Christmas, Addison and Dylan would visit Darling Bay to watch Earl, dressed up as Santa Claus, hand out gifts to the town's excited children. They'd enjoy the hokey apple-bobbing and square dancing in the town square, all decked out with holiday decorations, and spend time with the aunties. When Addison was feeling brave enough, they would gather wildflowers to place on Stephanie's grave in the small cemetery on a hill outside of town.

Dylan was a parenthesis in Addison's life. He represented dancing and music and glorious lovemaking, enlivening her otherwise dry, lawyerly existence. Dylan was...*fun*. But he wasn't—couldn't be—*the* one. How could she possibly show up to the firm's charity balls and corporate events with a bad-boy rocker on her arm? What chance would she have for a partnership at the firm with someone like Dylan by her side?

Besides, despite his protestations of eternal love for Addison, Dylan had replaced her in his life so fast it was downright insulting. Addison had seen the pictures on social media, those times when it was the middle of the night and she couldn't sleep. He was everywhere: Dylan with his band, Dylan with his guitar, Dylan with the beautiful, blonde, hometown Vivian.

Tears threatened, stinging the backs of Addison's eyes.

"What can't be cured must be endured," her mother used to say as she removed her apron and prepared to welcome Addison's Brownie troop for a weenie roast in the backyard.

Addison squared her shoulders, opened her ever-present notebook, and started a list.

1. Cancel hotel reservations
2. Change flight reservations
3. Re-pack for chilly weather
4. Buy presents for aunties
5. Find boyfriend

Number 5 was by far the most important, Addison thought. Because there was no way, no *way*, she would arrive in Darling Bay without a gorgeous, oh-so-eligible, man on her arm.

~

*D*ylan had received a letter, too. And he was stumped as to what to do about it.

He adored everything about Darling Bay: from the briny, fishy scents that blew in off the bay, to the whiff of eucalyptus and pine needles from the gently sloping hills, it was everything he hadn't even known he wanted until he saw it. Dylan had been raised in a transient, hardscrabble neighborhood of Houston, and when Addie first brought him to her little bayside hometown it was love at first sight: a picturesque small-town community where people looked out for each other that was still within reasonable driving distance of San Francisco. It was the kind of place a man could imagine settling down and raising a family.

But thinking about Darling Bay put him in mind of Addie, and that put him into a blind rage.

Because as quickly as Dylan had fallen in love with Darling Bay, he had fallen for Addie even faster.

Dylan had been assigned the label of the "bad kid" in high school, the kind parents told their children not to associate with. He wasn't sure why, exactly, and it had hurt. His reputation as a bad influence began about the time he fell in love with playing the guitar, and was solidified by a mean nicotine habit. He began hanging around outside the school gates after class, having a bit of a smoke, and the bad boy reputation soon followed. He wasn't in a gang, didn't break into houses or steal cars, didn't pick on little kids, take drugs or get in fights. *A regular Boy Scout,* Dylan thought with a wry smile. But the deal was sealed when he joined a band and started driving a motorcycle because he couldn't afford a car. Apparently it was a universal law that a cigarette-smoking, motorcycle-riding musician must be bad, and so suddenly Dylan was a bad boy.

Which, it turned out, was total chick bait. He had grown up as the only boy with four sisters and a strong mother. He loved women. And now they had started to love him back.

For years he traveled the country with his band, playing in dive bars as well as finer venues, meeting all kinds of people and having a whole lot of fun. And then he met Addison.

She had walked into a pub where his band was playing on Mission Street, in San Francisco. He was killing time at the bar until the band was scheduled to play and noticed her immediately: she stuck out in the rather seedy establishment in her nylons and dark jacket over a straight skirt, her honey-colored hair tied up in a loose knot on her head, small gold hoop earrings, low-heeled shoes, a heavy-looking, battered messenger bag slung across her chest. All buttoned up, and buttoned down, her body language said "back off." Their eyes met briefly, before she headed for a booth at the back the room.

He watched her throughout the evening's performance. She stayed in the booth huddled over a laptop and a bunch of papers, ignoring the increasingly raucous scene around her. Single minded. Focused. Every once in a while a strand of honey-brown hair escaped from her ponytail and she would tuck it behind her ear, oblivious to everyone and everything. The band was taking a break between sets when a drunk frat boy reeled over to her table and refused to leave her alone. So Dylan stepped in. Things ratcheted up quickly, and the drunk threw a punch. Dylan ducked it and punched back out of pure instinct. The man went down with a thud.

In the movies this sort of thing looked easy. In reality Dylan's hand exploded in pain, and all he could do was hope the man hadn't hit his head hard enough to have seriously hurt himself.

Luckily, the pub's bartender, Stan, was a friend. Stan and Dylan got the drunk to his feet, checked him out, declared him more affected by the liquor than the fight, and sat him down with a bag of frozen peas for his eye and a cup of coffee for his sobriety.

Someone tapped Dylan on the shoulder.

Up close all he noticed were her big hazel eyes shot through with blue and brown, high cheekbones, lips too full and sensuous to allow her to be overlooked. She wasn't model-beautiful, but there was something about her.... Dylan thought he caught a hint of subtle perfume, but perhaps it was his imagination: she *looked* like she smelled good.

"Thank you for being my knight in shining armor," she said with a crooked smile. She glanced at the ailing frat boy, still clutching the frozen peas. "Is he going to be all right?"

"He might have a shiner tomorrow," Dylan said. "But he'll be fine."

"Good. He was a creep, but I'd hate to see him hurt. I was just about to leave, but could I buy you a drink to thank you?"

"Sure, yeah. That'd be great."

"I'm betting you're a scotch man. Single malt?"

"Stan," Dylan called out to the bartender. "This beautiful woman wants to buy me a single malt scotch. I think I'm in love."

"You oughtta marry that woman," yelled Stan from down the bar.

"Excellent suggestion," said Dylan, and turned to Addison. "Woman, will you marry me? But first, tell me your name."

She laughed and held out her hand. "Addison McGee. And you are?"

"Dylan Madison. It's a pleasure."

He took her hand in his. As soon as their palms touched, an electric current ran through them. Their eyes met and held.

"Dylan *Madison*?" said Addison, after a beat. Her voice was hoarse with…what was it? Simple attraction, or something more? An overwhelming and completely surprising sense of rightness, of magic, of…home. "Well, Dylan, I hate to say this but the wedding's off."

"How so?"

"Addison Madison? Seriously?"

~

That was the first time Dylan asked Addie to marry him. It became a running joke throughout their relationship: "Woman, will you marry me?" he would say, often when she was annoyed with him, and they would laugh.

Right up until the moment the proposal was no longer a joke.

Last year, on Christmas Eve, in Darling Bay.

"You want me to *marry* you?" Addie had gasped. "I mean...for real?"

"Yes, for real," Dylan had said, unsure how to interpret Addie's look of shock. He was teetering on one knee, holding up a small black velvet box.

She gaped at him.

When Dylan had rehearsed the proposal scene in his mind, it had unfolded very differently. True, he was wearing his usual black leather jacket and jeans, and they were on a pier in Darling Bay's harbor, still redolent of the day's catch off the fishing boats. They had been on their way to dinner, and the sun was setting, turning the winter sky spectacular shades of orange and red, and it was Christmas Eve. It was their third Christmas together at Darling Bay, and though he had originally planned to pop the question after a romantic dinner, the moment had just seemed right.

"But...I'm a lawyer," Addie said. "A *New York City* lawyer."

"I know that. But surely you could find a position out here, maybe something in San Francisco? That way we could spend weekends in Darling Bay."

Addison couldn't believe her ears. How could Dylan be asking her to marry him, for real? More than that, how could he be asking her to move back to Darling Bay? To marry him, to have children...to become a mother? To become *her* mother.

Did he know her so little? Didn't Dylan understand that he didn't fit into the urbane, professional life she had envisioned for herself, had worked so hard to achieve?

Still. The thought of losing Dylan was…impossible. She couldn't just say *no*. Could she? It would be like losing a part of herself. The fun part of herself.

So in the end, Addie didn't answer. Instead she said, "I need a drink," and headed for the saloon, a confused Dylan trailing behind. She took a seat at the bar and began pounding who knows how many shots of tequila –on an empty stomach, which was never a good idea.

"So, you have an answer for me, woman?" He was trying to make his voice hold a joking tone, but she heard the seriousness underneath.

She raised another finger to the bartender. "One more tequila, Nate? Thanks."

The situation went from bad to worse the moment Vivian arrived. If it was possible for high schoolers to have a bête noir, Vivian Engel was Addison's. Vivian was everything Addison wasn't: popular, a cheerleader, Junior Prom Princess, the lead in the school play. Addison, in comparison, had been the president of the Honor Society, and had missed the Junior Prom because she was babysitting the Meyers kids to earn money for her college applications. Graceful Vivian was a trained dancer and a natural athlete; Addison tended to trip a lot.

On the evening Dylan proposed and meant it, Addison looked up over her tequila to see Vivian, in her adorable Santa's Elf get-up, hanging on Dylan, whispering in his ear, her body pressed against his. She was so close to him she could have lifted her mouth to his, and Dylan didn't even back up. Instead, his eyes danced as he looked down at her with a big smile. By morning, the entire town would know that the lovely and talented Vivian Engel had once again bested poor little book-smart Addison McGee.

Addison slammed her glass down on the bar, marched up to Smoke the firefighter, and said, "C'mon, big guy. We're going to dance."

She led Smoke onto the dance floor, the music changed to a slow dance, and Smoke wrapped his arms around her. She leaned into him and rested her head on his shoulder. She and Smoke had known each other since kindergarten; they even went to the Senior Prom together because neither of them had a date.

The slow dance was coming to an end when suddenly a hand landed on Smoke's shoulder, spun him around, and hit him with such force –and surprise—that the big man was knocked to the ground.

"What's your problem, man?" Smoke demanded as he got up. Dylan swung again, and missed. Soon punches were flying, and an all-out brawl ensued. Addison couldn't believe her eyes as Dylan—Dylan!—embarrassed her in front of the whole saloon.

Much later that night, Dylan had stormed out of Siren Song with the velvet box in his pocket and a cast on his arm, and Addison had fled back to New York City with her broken, aching heart.

And that had been that.

~

"I need a boyfriend," Addie said into the phone she clutched far too tightly against her ear.

"*Finally*," said her friend, Raquel, with a chuckle. "I've been telling you that for a year."

"Not a real boyfriend. A boy toy to accompany me to a command performance in Darling Bay."

"I thought you swore you were never going back there?"

"I did. And I meant it. But I pretty much have to go. Earl Pickett passed away, but before he did he sent me a personal invitation to his memorial service."

There was a brief pause. "So let me get this straight: You're pissed at this Earl fellow for messing up your holiday plans?"

"No, of course not, it's not that. But—"

"Addie, I say this as a friend: it's time to get your head out of your own butt. A man *died*. It's not all about you."

"I know, you're right." Until that moment Addison had pushed aside her feelings, afraid to confront the painful loss at Earl's passing. It seemed unreal, somehow, that old Earl wouldn't be there to greet her when she went home, standing on his doorstep, waving her into the warmth of his home, a fire roaring in the hearth, the muffled woof of his huge Great Dane named Gustavo.

Addison felt a deep-down, strangely detached sort of devastation, the same emotion she'd been experiencing ever since she and Dylan broke up. *It was all for the best*, she kept telling herself. But she wasn't buying it.

"I didn't mean to hurt your feelings," Raquel said. "I blame New York City. You've been there too long. Why don't you take that San Francisco job offer and come back to the Bay Area, where you belong? We miss you!"

"I miss you, too," Addison said with a pang. "But as

great as San Francisco is, it's just too close to Darling Bay. You're right, though. Not about New York—the city is great—but about me. I have been a little…self-absorbed lately." She paused. "Maybe a lot too self-absorbed lately."

"Remember how much you used to love volunteering? It might do you some good to get back out amongst those less fortunate."

"Hey, you should see the size of the check I cut last month for the Children's Defense League."

"Money's easy, if you have it. Time and heart are something else."

"True. Maybe I'll start volunteering again in the New Year. Or get therapy. Or both. Right this moment, though, I have a more immediate problem. Help me?"

"By finding you a fake boyfriend?"

"Bingo. Nothing unseemly or illegal—just someone to put his arm around me during a visit to Darling Bay and act like my boyfriend so I don't have to do this alone. I'll pay, whatever it takes. Preferably someone good-looking, and charming and smart and sweet…or at least able to pretend to be those last two."

"Let's see…"

"Gay would be good."

"Attractive, intelligent, and good-natured. Not to mention without plans for the holidays. And maybe gay. Anything else? Maybe the ability to turn water into wine or pull a sword out of a stone?"

"I know I'm asking a lot. But you're my only chance. You know all those fascinating artists and intellectuals in San Francisco—"

"What makes you think I'm not saving them for myself?"

"Because you're happily married?"

"Well, there is that. Hmm. Let me think…"

Addison waited, fiddling with the talisman Earl had tucked into the letter he sent. She was almost certain it had been made by her aunt Maisie. The supple leather and slick beads felt reassuring under her fingertips.

"One person comes to mind. James Culpepper. He's in the middle of a breakup, himself, and is desperate for a distraction over the holidays. He's a techie, but he—"

"Sounds perfect. Set us up?"

And so she had.

~

It wasn't until Addison found herself knocking on Earl's big oak door, half expecting the old man to greet her with his hearty: *Oh ho! It's my favorite courting couple!* that she thought to wonder who would answer now that Earl was gone. *Gone.* She still couldn't make herself believe it was true.

She heard Gustavo-the-dog's deep *woof*.

The door swung open.

Dylan.

Addison blinked, convinced she must be imagining him, seeing his features in the face of a stranger, as she frequently did. But this time the realism was stunning. He had aged in the time they had been apart: there were a few new grey hairs at his temple, the crinkles at the corners of his eyes were more pronounced—and more adorable—than before.

"*Addie.*" His voice washed over her.

As often as she envisioned him, his voice—his deep, velvety, caring voice—had never rung out with such clarity. It must be this place, she thought to herself. Why hadn't she rented a cheap motel room in Bodega Bay and driven the half hour to the memorial service? Why had she decided to stay at Earl's, in Darling Bay? In Siren Song cottage, no less, the magical place where she had once believed love to be real.

"Addie?" Dylan repeated. "Everything all right?"

"What the—?" Addie croaked, her voice scaling upward. *"What the hell are you doing here?"*

Dylan just smiled that funny little half-smile of his, his eyes never leaving Addie's, gazing at her as he always had, confusion vying with fascination, as if trying to figure her out, as if she were endlessly enthralling.

They stared at each other for a long moment, their eyes locked, surrounded by the tang of brine off the bay, the hoot of a faraway owl, the rustle of a small animal darting through the underbrush. Dylan's strong, graceful, guitar-playing hand rested on Gustavo's neck, stroking him absentmindedly, as the huge animal wagged his tail and crooned a hello, pleased to see Addison.

"Hey there, big guy," Addison murmured as she crouched down to hug Gustavo. The big dog wagged his tail, his reassuringly thick neck warm and soft, helping to ground her. She hadn't thought of it before, but the poor pup had lost his Earl. Who would take care of him now?

"Hi there!" James-the-fake-boyfriend joined them on

the porch of Earl's house. He set their luggage down and placed one hand on Addie's shoulder, reaching out the other to shake Dylan's hand in a "hale fellow, well met" gesture.

"James Culpepper. Pleased to meet you," he said cheerfully, then checked his phone.

Addison had breathed a sigh of relief when she rendezvoused with her mystery date at the San Francisco Airport. She should have known Raquel would come through. James Culpepper was exactly what Addie ordered: tall, broad-shouldered, lean but well-muscled. His hair was a gleaming dark gold, and he was dressed in a deep blue cashmere sweater that matched his eyes, topped by a sport coat. He had greeted her with a warm smile, and the sweet hug he'd given her had made her hope Raquel had pulled off getting her a gay fake-boyfriend.

Perfect, she thought. The photos of the two of them that she would post to social media would be perfect. Addison died a little more inside just thinking about it.

Speaking of dying....

When Dylan's dark eyes shifted from her to James, Addie felt like he had snatched away a warm blanket, plunging her back into an icy world devoid of passion and love and...Dylan.

"Nice to meet you," James persisted, his hand still held out. Dylan hadn't yet taken it. "I'm James Culpepper, Addie's boyfriend. And you are...?"

"Sorry," Dylan said, a curtain descending over his features. Addie wondered if he felt that same sheet of ice. "I'm Dylan Madison. I hadn't expected anyone this evening."

"What are you doing in Earl's house?" Addie demanded.

"I'm staying here for a few weeks."

"You're staying here?"

"Yes, I—"

"Wait, you're staying *here*?" Addie interrupted before he could finish his sentence.

James looked amused. "*Aha*, I'm a little late to the party, but should I assume you're Dylan, as in *the* Dylan? The Dylan who broke my sweet Addison's heart?"

Dylan's gaze once again met Addie's. The soft, searching look had been replaced by something as dark and bitter as the French Roast coffee they used to savor while lolling in bed, not thirty feet from here, in the magical Siren Song cottage.

"I think you've got that backwards, there, *James*," Dylan said, as if saying the other man's name hurt his tongue. "Addie broke my heart, not the other way around."

"I suppose that judgment is in the eye of the beholder, as they say," James replied with a still-hearty voice. He was playing his role exactly as Addie had asked him to on the long drive to Darling Bay. So why did every word feel like a knife stabbing her in the heart?

"I don't understand," Addison said. "I thought your band was playing in Cabo this weekend."

"They are," Dylan replied. He offered no further explanation.

"I just...I didn't think you would be here," Addison said.

"Well, that makes two of us. Earl said you weren't planning to come back for Christmas this year."

"Plans change. Anyway, what's done is done," Addison

said, trying to regroup. "So, you're staying in the front house?"

"You don't know?" Dylan asked.

"Know what?"

Dylan's impossibly dreamy eyes flickered over to James, then back to Addison. "Why don't we discuss the situation in the morning, over coffee. I imagine you're both pretty tired."

"Sounds like a plan," said James. "Could use some rest."

"What situation?" Addison said at the same time.

"Let's talk in the morning," Dylan insisted.

Addison did her best to unclench her jaw. She couldn't believe Earl would lie to her to bring her back to Darling Bay—okay, he hadn't *lied,* exactly, but he had apparently had some ulterior motive. And now she was standing here with hunky James's hand resting on her shoulder, which was driving her nuts, and gorgeous Dylan was standing in front of her, in his white T-shirt and faded jeans, looking good enough to eat with a spoon.

Driving her nuts in an entirely different way.

"All right, fine," said Addison. "I guess James and I will just go on back to Siren Song, then."

There was another long pause, another long gaze as Dylan seemed to assess first her, and then James. Then, with a brisk nod, Dylan reached around to the side of the door and snatched the Siren Song key off the hook.

"I believe you know the way," he said as he held the key out to her.

"Of course," she said, and he dropped the key in her open palm as though avoiding her touch.

"Good night, Gustavo," she said. "Nice to see you, big guy."

Before stepping off the porch Addison couldn't resist one final dig at Dylan:

"I hope you're not headed over to the saloon to start yet another brawl."

Dylan grinned. "Only time I'm in bar fights is when you're around."

"Hey, don't blame me for your bad behavior," she replied. "*You're* the one who attacked poor Smoke last year."

"Funny you should mention that," said Dylan, leaning against the doorjamb and crossing his arms over his chest. "Smoke has become a good friend."

Nerves danced along her skin. "Is that right? And just how long have you been in town?"

"A few days. But I've visited a few times over the last year." In fact, Dylan had come back to Darling Bay last New Year's Eve to make amends for starting the brawl, paying for the mirror at the saloon and apologizing to Smoke. Smoke wasn't one to hold a grudge, and had invited Dylan to go fishing the next day. Dylan took him up on the offer and had stayed in Earl's spare room. The rock 'n' roller and the elderly war veteran spent the evening sipping Earl's favorite brandy and swapping stories by the fire. Since then Dylan had returned to Darling Bay regularly. He found comfort in the town's slow pace, the friendly smiles, the memories of Addie, and helping Earl with his chores.

"You seem to have made yourself at home," Addison

said, annoyed that Dylan seemed to have been accepted in the town, in *her* town.

"What can I say? I'm a likeable guy. I make friends easily." Then he added in a voice just above a murmur. "Unlike some people."

Addison let out a rude snort. "Yeah, I've seen the photos of you and Vivian. You two looked pretty friendly, indeed."

"You know, Addison," James intervened, giving her shoulder a gentle squeeze. "I would love to get settled in for the evening. It's late."

"Oh, I…of course," said Addison, trying to mask her surprise at James's touch. She kept forgetting about him. Dylan was all she could see. "Good night."

Dylan nodded, watched the couple walk away, and slowly shut the door.

He turned to Gustavo. "So, who the hell is this *'James'* person?"

Gustavo looked up at him and wagged his tail.

Dylan let out a long, harsh breath as he headed to the liquor cabinet to pour himself a drink. "Merry fricking Christmas to you, Madison. You poor, lovelorn, sucker."

Gustavo woofed his agreement.

~

Walking into Siren Song was even worse than being greeted by Dylan instead of Earl, and Addison kicked herself for not staying somewhere else—even the cheapest motel room would have been better than this.

The beautiful little place held too many memories of

happiness, of love. She had the wrong man by her side as she took in the little gingham curtains, the tiny café table and coffee service set out on the small counter. The loveseat and comfy overstuffed armchair faced a large window, the grouping brought together by a large, blue-and-white braided oval rug. What had once felt so perfect, so right, now evoked a pervasive sense of *wrongness* that she couldn't shake.

"I need a drink," Addison said. "How about you?"

She was actively trying not to see, not to feel. *All you have to do is make it through Sunday*, Addison told herself. But even that simple goal was feeling less and less realistic.

"Unless you're packing some booze we'd have to go out," James said as he set their bags inside the door. "I'm game if you are, but didn't you tell me that caused trouble the last time you were here?"

On the hour-long drive from the airport to Darling Bay, Addison had learned that James was an ex-startup guy, after selling his app, GreenYo, for approximately a zillion dollars. He had accepted her unorthodox offer to pretend to be her boyfriend for the weekend because he'd lost a bet with Raquel's daughter. He said he liked a little adventure. James was nice and polite, if a bit distant, and as far as she could tell from their brief time together they didn't have much in common. James also had a habit of obsessively checking and rechecking his cell phone. It was starting to annoy Addison, but under the circumstances she kept her mouth shut. James was doing her a huge favor, after all.

"Yeah, I suppose you're right," Addison said. She wasn't in the mood to face the crowd at the saloon just yet, anyway. "A shower, then. I'm going to take a long, hot shower."

"Sounds good," James said as he checked out the cottage's amenities: the teensy closet, the bathroom with its white bead board and white porcelain fixtures, fluffy towels neatly stacked on the shelves. He climbed the ladder to peek at the loft.

Addison felt suffocated by her clothes. She unbuttoned her wool blazer and silk shirt and unzipped her pencil skirt. James descended the ladder and halted abruptly on the last step, lifting his eyebrows.

"Oh. Sorry. Forgot where I was," Addison said, seeing his look. "If it makes you uncomfortable, I'll change in the bathroom."

"That might be for the best," James said. "What do you want to do about the sleeping arrangements? I couldn't help notice there's only one bed."

"I know, I'm sorry."

"Um. Were we supposed to share, then?"

"Would that bother you?" She asked, a bit surprised. She and Smoke once shared a tent on a camping trip in high school. What was the big deal?

"It's just...I suppose we could do the rolled-up towel thing, or something. Maybe hang a sheet, like in that old movie—*It Happened One Night*?"

She stared at him, the truth sinking in. "But... I guess I assumed you were gay!" Addison protested, hastily pulling on her robe.

"Why?"

She waved a hand. "The cashmere..."

"I like good clothes. Some straight men do."

"But you've seen me in my… *altogethers!*"

James smiled. "Your what, now?"

"That's what my aunties call undergarments."

"Ah."

"And I was hoping to set you up with Smoke."

"Isn't he your ex's best friend?"

"Well, obviously I didn't realize that at the time. But at least he's gay."

"I apologize for not being gay."

"It's all right. Not your fault. Water under the bridge, and all that." Addison's mind was racing. Sharing a bed with a not-gay virtual stranger was not in her comfort zone. The love seat wasn't nearly long enough to sleep on, but she could make up a pallet with the cushions and sleep on the floor. It was only for a few nights, after all. The important thing was that no one learn that she and James weren't the couple she wanted everyone to believe they were.

Another reason she had asked Raquel to find her a gay fake boyfriend was so she wouldn't have to contend with hormones or expectations of intimacy. But as she watched James's handsome face as he settled into the armchair and checked his cell phone, she realized: it didn't matter that James was straight. He seemed like a decent guy, but he wasn't Dylan.

Stop it, Addison scolded herself. *Dylan betrayed you, remember? First by not being what you need, then by walking away just like Dad did. Not to mention embarrassing you in front of everybody with the lovely Vivian.* And the worst betrayal of all: he had moved on with his life while Addison was still dead inside.

When she pulled out her toiletries bag, Auntie Maisie's leather-and-bead talisman fell out onto the counter. Addison took a moment to stroke it, focusing on her breathing.

Sunday, Addison reminded herself. All you have to do is make it through Sunday.

~

"Let's go to the Golden Spike Café for breakfast," suggested Addison to James the next morning.

Siren Song had a tiny kitchenette stocked with coffee and tea, and before Earl got sick he used to leave a basket of fresh baked goods at the door. But Addison was in a hurry to leave. Lingering in Siren Song with James, even if just for coffee, felt wrong.

"Sounds good," James said. He was wearing khakis and a different cashmere sweater, and looked fresh as a daisy after his night in the loft sleeping on the most comfortable bed in the world. Addison, on the other hand, was bleary-eyed from her makeshift accommodations. She stared at the contents of her suitcase, wondering what to wear. Her last-minute change of holiday plans hadn't allowed time to shop for something more suitable to Darling Bay, and so she had mostly packed city clothes. She sighed and took out a nice black wool short skirt and matching jacket over a red silk knit shell, tights, and tall boots. She hurried into the bathroom to change.

James continued, "But are you sure you're okay sleeping on the floor? We could probably get a cot or something—"

"*No*," she said, shaking her head as she emerged from

the bathroom and grabbed her purse. They walked out of the cottage and into a damp, chilly morning. Their shoes rapped smartly on the wooden deck that connected Siren Song to Earl's house and from there to the street. "Thanks. But word would get out, and that would defeat the whole purpose of your being here."

"Which is to make Dylan Madison jealous."

"Exactly. I mean, no! No, of course not. I didn't even know Dylan was going to be here when I asked you to be my date."

"Okay. But then why *am* I here?"

"I didn't want to show up in town alone."

James gave her a sidelong glance as they walked up the road toward Darling Bay's small Main Street. The air smelled of eucalyptus and salt. James checked his phone before sliding it into his pocket.

"I might be overstepping my role as your fake boyfriend, Addison, but you're a smart, independent woman. And these are your childhood friends and neighbors, aren't they? Why do you feel you can't come home without a man on your arm?"

"Just…because," she said.

"But don't—"

"I don't want to talk about it," Addison said. "Just because, okay?"

Because she was still mortified by what happened last year. Because she couldn't bear to face the looks—not of anger, but of sympathy—that she knew she would encounter from the hometown folks. Because she couldn't bear to think of herself in Darling Bay without Dylan by her side.

And because Dylan had betrayed her.

James nodded, and to change the subject—and to distract herself—Addison launched into her tour guide guise, pointing out the plaque commemorating the founding of Darling Bay, the Crab's Claw and the bagel shop, the pier that stretched far out into the water with its wire Christmas tree sitting right out at the very end.

James made appropriate, polite comments as they toured the small town before coming to a halt and saying "Coffee? Please?"

"This way," she laughed, and headed to the café.

Addison took a deep breath as James reached for the door handle.

"Ready?" he asked softly. "You can do this."

She nodded and they stepped into the lively restaurant.

Conversations that had bubbled and swirled throughout the diner screeched to a halt. An excruciating silence descended as all and sundry turned to gape at Addison standing at the entrance with a strange man on her arm.

Norma was on a stool, Bloody Mary in her left hand and what looked like some kind of spindle in her right. Lana Darling was sitting with her sister Adele in a booth, chatting and laughing as their other sister, Molly, spun past with the coffee pot. Tox and Coin, two of the firefighters from Station One, stood next to the cash register as Nikki handed them a white bag.

Everyone stared.

For a moment Addison felt once again the awkwardness of the child whose father had left her, the unwanted kid with the mother who did her duty with grim determination but would never hug her or make silly jokes like the other moms did. The straight-A nerd everyone in town complimented but secretly pitied, who walked around with her nose in a book because most of her friends were fictional.

"Show 'em who's boss, kid," James murmured in her ear.

Addison nodded. Why was she feeling this way? She wasn't a lonely outcast anymore. She had worked hard and was an unqualified success: a hotshot New York lawyer who was at ease conversing with Wall Street's doers and shakers at fundraising dinners and corporate shindigs. She lifted her chin, threw back her shoulders, and pasted a smile on her face.

"Merry Christmas, everyone," she said in a loud voice. "So nice to see you all! I'd like to introduce James Culpepper, my boyfriend."

A few people called out a greeting, while others sketched a wave or nodded. Things went back to normal, and Addison took a second to take it all in—this was home, after all. She'd grown up in and out of this place, and while it looked *way* better than it had when she was a kid— cleaner and brighter—it still retained its down-home charm. Overhead, colorful surfboards dangled from fisherman's rope. Crab pots held extra coffee pots. The tables shone with use, as did the shiny wooden floor.

"Good to see you, Addison," said Molly Darling as Addison led James to an empty table by the window. "Merry Christmas."

"You sure do look like a New Yorker!" said Norma, taking in the expensive wool suit that made Addison stick out like a primrose among the poppies. "Like you should be getting out of a yellow cab. I took one of them once, right through the city. Fellow went about a hundred miles an hour and then refused to let me out till I laughed at one of his jokes." She sucked down more of her Bloody Mary.

"Hey, you! Have you seen your aunts yet?" asked Lana as they passed by,

"Soon," Addison said. Her heart sank as she realized that fooling the townsfolk was one thing but fooling the aunties was quite another. They would no doubt take one look at James and know something was off. Willa had The Eye, Maisie would try to use her pendulum on them, Clara would suggest a Tarot reading, and Minerva would insist on interpreting their tea leaves.

This was going to be a disaster.

All you have to do is make it through Sunday, Addison repeated what was quickly becoming her mantra. As if reading her mind, James squeezed her elbow and nodded encouragingly.

They sat and the waitress, Nikki McMurtry, came over.

"Happy holidays! Well, if it isn't Addison McGee!" Nikki exclaimed as she poured coffee for them, blatantly checking out James from under long lashes.

"And with such a nice-looking new boyfriend! What can I get ya, handsome?" she asked him with a wink.

He gave her a slow, delicious smile. "Well now, seeing as how I'm new in town perhaps you could recommend something?"

"A big boy like you, I'd go with the Monday Morning special. We call it that even though we offer it every day of the week. Hotcakes *and* eggs *and* bacon *and* sausage *and* homemade biscuits with jam. Hard to beat."

"Sounds great," James agreed. "Monday Morning Special it is."

"And for you, Addison? Half a grapefruit or maybe some toast?"

"I'll have the special as well," said Addison, though she never ate much for breakfast. Once in a while she did the New York City thing of grabbing a bagel and coffee to eat while walking to work, but usually breakfast was just a protein shake. But Addison was in a contrary mood, and Nikki's assumption that she wouldn't want a big breakfast annoyed her. Also, she wanted to get rid of Nikki quickly.

Addison slapped her menu shut, grabbed James's, and handed both over.

"Okay, sure thing," said Nikki, as she tucked the menus under her arm, made a note on her pad, and returned to the kitchen to place the order.

"Addison," James said softly. "It's okay. You're doing great. Try to relax. Hope you're hungry."

Addison smiled. James was a nice man, she thought. Too bad he was the *wrong* man. On the ride to Bolinas she had tried to ask him about his own recent breakup, curious about why he had been open to her unorthodox proposition. But James had played his cards close to his chest, and since she hadn't really felt like talking, either, the conversation hadn't gone very far after getting down the basics of his role as fake boyfriend. He'd merely said he was just fine, thanks.

"Hi, Addison, Merry Christmas! Have you seen the aunties yet?" Marsha Wiggins asked.

"We're going over there later today," Addison replied. "Merry Christmas to you, too. Oh hey, do you know if

Karen's boutique is open? I didn't have time to shop before I came; I need something more appropriate to wear, like jeans and a flannel shirt."

"No, sorry, honey. Karen's out of town for the holiday, visiting her daughter and grandkids in Sacramento. You might be able to talk Sam into opening up for you, though."

Just then Dylan walked in. Addison cursed herself for giving away the menus, so she didn't even have anything to hide behind.

Coming to the café had been a mistake. She should have known better than to remain stationary for long. She was a sitting duck.

Dylan crossed the café slowly, stopping to greet one person after another, shaking hands, wishing everyone a Merry Christmas and asking Norma about her sciatica. At long last—after Norma gave him many details—he reached their table.

"Good morning," Dylan said. "I trust you had a good night."

"Tell me something," Addison said. "I grew up in this town, not you. How is it that you act as if you belong here?"

"It's a friendly place, Addie. Remember? You told me that the first time we came."

"It's one thing to be friendly, quite another to treat the man who started a brawl in the saloon as if he's the mayor or something."

Dylan grinned and took a seat at the table.

"*Excuse* me," said Addison, lifting her eyebrows. "I don't recall inviting you to breakfast."

"Sorry if I'm interrupting," Dylan said, "but we need to talk."

"Don't let me stop you," James said, standing. "I need to check my messages, anyway. I'll just step outside for a moment."

"You don't have to…" Addison began, but he was gone.

Dylan's gaze followed James out the door. "Phone surgically attached, is it? I remember what that was like with you—always on your cell."

"I wasn't that bad."

He raised his eyebrows, but said nothing.

"Really? I was that bad?"

Dylan signaled to Nikki for a cup of coffee.

"I'm sorry. I know I can be a little…"

"High strung? Ambitious? Anal?"

"Type-A, I was going to say. Show me a successful lawyer who isn't."

"Now that, I'll grant you," he said. "Though to be honest, you're the only lawyer I know."

"Well, now, that's not entirely true. What about that nice young public defender who got the charges against you and the band dropped that time in San Antonio? Charges which were well founded, as I recall."

Dylan let out a whoop of laughter, and just about everybody in the café turned to stare. Addison had long ago learned to stifle the impulse to blush, and she lowered her eyes, studying the way her cream swirled in her coffee.

"I had forgotten about that," Dylan said, still chuckling. "Good times."

"Anyway, Dylan." Addison tried to pull herself together, ignoring how the sound of his laugh warmed her to her core, how the little crinkles at the edges of his eyes enchanted her, how just the sight of him made her want him, desperately want him, in some dark, secret, denied part of herself. "What is it that you want to talk about? Surely you don't want to—"

"It's Earl's place," Dylan interrupted her.

"What about it?"

"It's ours now."

"Beg pardon?"

"Earl left his place to us. Fifty-fifty split, you and me."

Addison froze, the coffee cup halfway to her mouth. "That's not possible."

"It's not only possible, it's real. Earl's nephew, Preston, was the executor of the will. He told me Earl's house, including Siren Song, was left to the two of us in joint tenancy, at least I think that's the phrase you lawyers use."

"That's the right phrase," Addie said, stunned by this revelation.

"But of more immediate concern is Gustavo."

Addie's heart sank even further. "Don't tell me."

"Shared custody."

"But, what does he…what *did* he…" Addison sputtered. "What in the world was Earl thinking?"

"You know exactly what he was thinking," Dylan said, his gaze flickering over to the door, as though checking for James's return. "We both do: Earl thought if he could manipulate us into spending time together then we would see the error of our ways and live happily ever after. With Gustavo, of course."

She let out an exasperated sound. "Well, that's just ridiculous."

Dylan seemed to hesitate for a moment before nodding in agreement.

"What I mean is," Addison clarified, "That was sweet of Earl, I guess, but emotions don't work that way. Besides, what does *Vivian* think of such an arrangement?"

"I haven't asked her," he said with a barely-there smile.

"Maybe you should. Is she with you this holiday season?"

"How do you know about Vivian?" he asked, seeming amused. "You've been spying on me?"

"Of course not. Some photos just happened to come up on my social media." She hadn't thought of it until this moment: of *course* Dylan was coming regularly to Darling Bay; he came to visit Vivian.

"Uh huh," he said, clearly unconvinced. Suddenly businesslike, Dylan asked, "So, any thoughts on how best to handle our interesting situation?"

"I, um...why are you asking me? This is the first I've heard of it. What do *you* think we should do?"

He shrugged. "Me? I'm just an itinerant rock 'n' roll musician. You're the bigshot city lawyer."

"I'm no expert in estate law. Much less canine custody precedents."

"So don't think like a lawyer. How about thinking like a human being? Your friend just died and left you part of a home, a business, and a dog. What does your common sense suggest?"

"I guess we could sell it. Not Gustavo, of course."

"You ready to say goodbye forever to Siren Song? Hand it over to a stranger? Just like that?"

"Well, no, but..."

"Look, Addie, you're the one with the family connections to Darling Bay. If you want, I'll walk away, simple as that," Dylan offered, his eyes searching her face.

"That doesn't seem fair. Earl wanted you to benefit, too."

"Then buy me out."

"Buy you...? But I don't want to run Siren Song! I live in New York City, remember?"

"Don't see as how I can forget," he said, his eyes sweeping over her business suit. "But we need to figure this out, Addie. When Earl got sick he didn't have the energy to do routine maintenance, nor the money to hire someone else to do it. You know better than I do that salt air plays hell with wooden buildings, and the place is starting to fall apart. If you really don't want any part of it, then I'd like to talk about buying *you* out."

"Buy *me* out? You want to live in Darling Bay, full-time?"

He nodded.

"But.... How?" She sputtered. "You don't have any money."

Dylan's jaw clenched, and she read anger in his dark eyes. Money had been a sore point between them once Addie graduated from law school and started earning a handsome salary from the firm. Dylan earned enough as a musician to get by, but it seemed to Addie that he spent every penny he took in. "Enough is good enough," seemed to be his motto. Addison had grown up without much in Darling Bay, and she had been determined to do well. Very well. New York-style well.

"You're right that I don't make the kind of money you

do, Addie. But I have some savings. I'd pay over time. With interest, of course. Draw up any kind of contract, and I'll sign it."

"You seriously have it?" She couldn't keep the surprise out of her voice.

"I've been saving every dime from every gig. Had a few songs go viral. I've been marketing on the internet, and teaching lessons. I've got a nest egg. Not enough to buy you out all at once, but it's enough to do some necessary renovations to Earl's house. I can open two more guest rooms as vacation rentals, in addition to Siren Song."

Addie sat still, stunned.

"And I've been offered a job teaching music for the local school district, and I was planning to offer private guitar lessons. I don't need much here."

"I don't..." Addie shook her head.

Nikki arrived with the food, setting one plate in front of Addison, the other in front of James's still-empty chair. *Where* was *James?* Addison glanced over at the door. *What good was a fake boyfriend who was constantly running off at crucial moments?*

Dylan studied the huge plate of food in front of Addison: the glistening bacon and sausage and fried eggs, the mountain of pancakes, the steaming biscuit dripping with butter.

"Planning on felling a few trees later?" he asked. "Maybe hoe the back forty?"

"Very funny," Addison said, though she regretted ordering all this food. What was with her today?

"Seriously, though. I don't remember you eating big breakfasts. You never used to like eggs."

"I'm trying something new," Addie replied, dunking a piece of her biscuit into the egg yolk, though she had no appetite. She popped the bread into her mouth, willing herself to chew.

"Addie," Dylan said softly, just loud enough for her to hear. "What the hell are you doing?"

He wasn't talking about the food. Neither was he talking about James, who had finally come back into the café and was making his way across the room toward them. Addie knew what he meant: Dylan was talking about the truth. About the fact that she was a wreck, that she wanted nothing more than to burst into tears, to ask her aunties for advice, to bury her face in Gustavo's neck and tell him she was so, so sorry about Earl.

Dylan knew. The way he always knew.

"Sorry about that," James said as he took his chair, wrapping his arm around Addison and squeezing her shoulder. "Well, I must say, this looks delicious. Care to join us, Dylan?"

"No, thank you," Dylan responded. "I've already eaten."

"You're not trying to horn in on my girl, here, are you?" James asked with a smile.

Dylan's eyes didn't leave Addison's face. "No. No, I'm not."

"Good thing," said James, spreading his napkin on his lap, picking up his fork, and digging into the huge plate of food. He made little "*mmmm*" sounds that set Addie's teeth on edge.

Her stomach careened wildly between vague nausea and butterflies at having Dylan so near. In New York, she was known for her cool head in the boardroom, not to mention the courtroom. What in the world was *wrong* with her?

"I'll leave you two to enjoy your breakfast," Dylan said, standing. "Addie, think about what we were discussing, and let me know what you decide."

Addison watched as Dylan stooped to pick up old Mrs. Haggerty's napkin, then lingered for a moment to chat with Nikki. Then he sidled out the door.

"You say Dylan's not from here?" James said as he slathered his biscuit with jam and took a huge bite. "He sure seems at home."

"Yes, doesn't he?" Addison shook her head in disbelief.

"What did he want to talk to you about? Getting back together? Has our ruse worked its magic already?"

"Not exactly, no."

James checked his phone.

"Is that absolutely necessary?" Addison demanded, irked.

"Is *what* absolutely necessary?"

"The constant checking of the phone."

He gave her a chagrined smile and put the phone away. "Sorry."

Addison could feel herself pursing her lips, a habit her mother had always insisted would give her "old lady wrinkles." She reminded herself: James was a nice man who was gamely doing what she had asked of him. He was perfect. He looked the part and he—other than the cell phone thing—*acted* the part. It wasn't his fault he was all wrong.

"So, what's next on the agenda?" he asked.

"We have a date with my aunties," Addison said, her

stomach kicking up again. "And before that, I was hoping to track down a man named Sam to buy some flannel."

"I'm sorry?"

"The clothes I brought with me aren't cutting it. I don't know what I was thinking. I already feel out of place, and these clothes…" she shrugged. "I grew up here, I know better. My friend Karen's shop is closed for the holiday, but if I can find Sam I can probably talk him into letting me in."

"To buy some flannel?"

"Exactly. And jeans. Oh, and some shoes."

"Sam sells all that, does he?"

"It's a general store. It sells a bit of everything, as long as you're not too picky."

"The wonder of small town life," James said, starting in on the pancakes. "And in the evening?"

"You know…" Addison said. Things were already feeling awkward with James; the prospect of spending every second of the next twenty-four hours together was beginning to feel overwhelming. "You probably have some business or personal things to take care of. Want to have the evening to yourself?"

"Sounds good to me," he said, amenable as always.

Addison had abandoned the breakfast and was nursing her coffee. Nikki came by to refresh her cup, and cooed her concern that Addison wasn't eating her breakfast.

Addison daydreamed about being in New York, where no one cared if she was eating all her food.

And where Dylan didn't haunt her around every corner.

~

*D*ylan left the saloon, closing the door with exaggerated care because the alternative was slamming it shut so hard the glass would shatter.

What in the hell are you doing, Madison?

There had to be a million small towns in this great country where he could put down roots, where he could build a life. Why, then, had he fixated on Darling Bay, a place where Addie was guaranteed to show up from time to time to visit her aunties? Yes, Darling Bay was special, but so were lots of places where he wouldn't face the heartache, the disruption that would naturally ensue each time Addie appeared on the scene.

And who the hell was this *James* character?

Dylan's humor wasn't helped any by the fact that he'd been up much of the night, tossing and turning, picturing James holding Addie in his arms, putting his mouth on her, in that enormous loft bed stuffed with angel feathers or whatever the hell it was that made it so inviting.

How could Addie have brought another man into their bed?

So this morning Dylan had gone to the saloon for much-needed caffeine and protein, but that plan had been foiled the moment he laid eyes on Addie and her boy toy. He couldn't bear to see the happy couple any more than necessary.

It gave Dylan a mean sense of satisfaction that the man kept checking his cell phone. He wondered if it made Addie feel like James was looking for someone, or something, more interesting. He hoped it annoyed her to no end.

Dylan walked down to the boardwalk. The marina was locking itself down for the storm—sailors hurried to batten down the hatches so they wouldn't fly open during the winds, and the fishing boats put out extra bumpers. Jake Ballard gave a quick wave as he pulled on some rope—no, make that line. Jake had been teaching him how to sail, even though Dylan never got the sailing terms right.

Yes, Darling Bay was special, but no matter how comfortable he felt here, how easily he had fallen into the habit of buying groceries at Martha's Market and how quickly he had gotten to know some of the town elders, he should probably find a different town to call his own.

"Hey, Madison!"

Dylan turned around to see Smoke climbing out of his huge white pickup truck. Smoke was huge, several inches over six feet tall, and built like a linebacker. He had a slow, thoughtful way of speaking, and the gentlest eyes in the world.

"What's up, Smoke?"

"I hear Addie's back in town for Christmas," Smoke said. He came to stand with Dylan on the boardwalk, his big boots making the wood creak companionably underneath them. Dylan could only imagine how reassuring it would be, if you were trapped in a fire, to see Smoke arrive to rescue you. Hard to believe he had ever been drunk enough, and jealous enough, to punch a man as big—and as sweet—as Smoke. Nothing, and no one, drove him crazy like Addie.

"Yes. Yes, she is," said Dylan.

"You okay?"

"Not really. But I'm working on it."

"Rumor mill says she's got a new man with her."

Dylan nodded.

"Sorry, man," Smoke said, frank sympathy in his eyes. "Anything I can do?"

"Want to go fishing?"

"You want to reconsider that?" Smoke gestured to the water.

"I suppose you're right," Dylan said, looking out across the water to the western horizon. The climate in Darling Bay was relatively temperate, but in the winter fierce storms would blow in from the Pacific Ocean, turning the placid waters of the bay into a roiling cauldron, downing power lines on land and, occasionally, dumping enough rain to cause landslides that cut the town off from the outside world for long days at a time.

"It's not exactly fishing, but I'm headed over to the fire station to wrap gifts for the Toys for Tots drive. Wanna help? Might get your mind off things."

"You've got yourself a deal," said Dylan. He couldn't vouch for his ability to tie ribbons into bows, but he was a whiz with wrapping paper and Scotch tape. He'd try anything if it got his mind off Addie. "Okay if I bring Gustavo along?"

"Sure! Gustavo's always welcome down at the station. And Vivian said she'd bring her guitar and play a few songs to keep us entertained."

"Vivian?" Dylan asked.

"In her Santa's Elf costume, no less."

"Let's go wrap some toys."

"Addie!" cried Willa, as all four aunties fluttered out onto the porch.

"Oh, sweet girl!" said Clara.

"Addie, how wonderful!" cooed Maisie.

Nothing like coming to the aunts' house to make Addison feel special. At first. Before the itching-to-get-away set in.

The aunties—officially, they were Stephanie's aunts, which made them Addison's *great* aunts—lived in a big old farmhouse painted a sunny yellow that sat just outside of town. The house had been built long ago in a clearing in the middle of the forest. The aunts had nursed the remnants of an old peach orchard and each summer tended verdant vegetable gardens. They coaxed potted flowers all year around.

After her father left them, Stephanie and Addison had lived in a series of characterless rentals, and so the big yellow farmhouse had come to mean home to her. This was where she had experienced cinnamon-scented hugs and exorbitant praise and soft laps, where she had been encouraged to climb trees and try her hand at baking and to join in off-key renditions of Motown classics that echoed down the halls.

This house had been Addison's port in the storm, her safe haven. Stephanie had considered the aunties stark-raving crazy—"merely eccentric," Maisie insisted with a smile—but as far as Addison was concerned, they were enchanting.

And they were smart. Maybe more than smart—*super-*

naturally smart. The aunties believed in magic.

Addison had been trained intellectually not to believe in such things, but there was no denying that the older women sometimes knew things they shouldn't know. On the other hand, Darling Bay's gossip network was impressive, indeed, so perhaps they were merely privy to more information than she.

After greeting James with effusive hugs, the aunties hurried the couple into the house to get out of the weather, which was turning blustery and threatening rain. The house was packed with heavy wooden furniture and polished built-ins; the walls lined with shelves crowded with books and mementos and sundry knick-knacks. There were also several cats and one extremely old, three-legged Chihuahua named Miss Idaho.

The house smelled like Christmas.

"Something sure smells delicious," said James.

"Are you baking your German cookies?" Addison asked, inhaling deeply of baking spices and sugar, overlaid with the pine scent from the massive Christmas tree in the front window.

"Of course!" replied Willa. The aunties were descended from solid English stock, but somewhere in her travels Willa had learned how to make German pastries, and always baked them for the holidays. Dozens and dozens of spritzkuchen, lebkuchen and pfeffernusse, stolle and streusel. Far too many for family and friends to eat, so she would drop them off at schools and fire-houses, and distribute them to shut-ins and anyone who seemed in need of a homemade treat. Her whole life, when Addie smelled nutmeg and ginger and cinnamon, she would be transported back to Christmas at this farmhouse.

"Addie," said Clara after they were all ensconced in the massive kitchen. "Won't you come with me for just a moment? I wanted to ask you about a few things of your mother's."

"Oh, of course." Addison glanced at James. "You all right here?"

He gave her a reassuring smile. "I've been promised fresh baked goods. I'm a very happy man."

Clara led the way into the library. Addison paused in front of a large framed portrait of her mother, which had been taken when Stephanie was about Addison's age now.

"I look so much like her," Addison said.

Clara nodded. "You always have. Oh, here's what I wanted you to look through—I thought about sending them to you in New York, but I feared they would get lost in the mail."

In the corner were a few small boxes of mementos left-over from when Stephanie had moved in with the aunties, after she got sick.

"You shouldn't have had to save all this for me. I'm sure there's nothing valuable in here, but it was sweet of you to keep it," said Addison, poking through old cards, a few letters, junk jewelry, and a number of small crafts she had made in a vain bid for her mother's affection. Addison picked up a lumpy coiled ceramic bowl she had made in summer camp. She weighed it in her hands, running her fingertips over the shiny slickness of the ugly purple glaze. She couldn't believe her mother had kept it.

Addison looked up to find Clara's eyes on her.

"I guess that bowl was important enough to keep, at least to Stephanie. Sometimes we don't always keep exactly what we need to, so she was lucky," Clara said. "Addie, would you like me to read your tarot? You and James?"

"*No*, no thank you," said Addison hastily. "Listen, Clara, I know you all mean well but I really don't want you to do any magic around James, okay?"

"Of course, sweetheart. Who would think of such a thing?"

But when they returned to the kitchen, James was not only eating cake but there was a teapot on the table.

"Aunt Minerva, what are you doing?" Addison demanded.

"Oh, nothing, dear," Minerva said as she brazenly swirled the tiniest last bit of tea around in James's discarded cup.

James didn't notice, as he was busy checking his phone for messages.

"Did you even *ask* James if he wanted you to read his tea leaves?" Addison demanded.

"Well honestly, Addie," said Clara. "Who wouldn't want their tea leaves read? You'd have to pay good money for this sort of thing at the carnival, and then it's rarely done right. You know as well as I do that Minerva reads the leaves with remarkable clarity."

"This can be a very personal thing," Addie insisted. "I don't think—"

James looked up and chuckled. "It's fine, Addie, thanks. So, what do you see, Aunt Minerva?"

"The letter J. Does that mean anything to you?"

James shrugged and shook his head, but seemed mildly intrigued.

"A woman's name, I think. Joanie...? Josie, maybe?"

The smile on James's face stilled. "Did you say Josie? That's funny, I met a Josie this morning when I got a muffin."

"Wait, you got a muffin? We went to breakfast together!"

James said, "I get up at five. You were boring this morning, all snores and mumbling. But come on, Josie's a common name."

Aunt Minerva raised one eyebrow and peered more deeply into the cup. "She seems to be looking for something, or someone. You know in the movie, *The Wizard of Oz*, where Dorothy is looking for her aunt, or her home, is it? Or maybe her dog? I forget, but Josie's face reminds me of that. Like she's lost, and she's looking for—"

"What else does it say?" James demanded, suddenly intent.

"Something about a bill."

He leaned forward. "A bill? For what?"

Aunt Minerva said, "No, paper money, I mean. A large bill, passed to someone who didn't want it."

"A fifty?"

Minerva slanted her gaze to him. "Perhaps. And I hear a phrase: *going off the market.* That mean anything to you?"

James pushed back from the table, jumping to his feet so quickly that the chair teetered and threatened to fall. "That's enough," he said. "I'm sorry, but that's...that's enough. Excuse me, I need to step outside for a moment."

He headed for the front door, his phone already held to his ear.

The aunties watched him rush out into the wind and rain, closing the door behind him. In unison, they turned to Addison.

"Really, Addie?" Clara said, looking sympathetic.

"What in the world is going on, sweetheart?" asked Willa.

"That poor man's about to fall in love," Maisie nodded. "But not with you."

"And *you're* already in love," Minerva added in, "But not with him."

"That's a fine mess you've gotten yourself into," Clara summed up.

"My goodness, what *is* it with the four of you all?" asked Addison. "I adore you all, my dear aunts, but you're like a Greek chorus sometimes. Not everything is 'seeable', you know. Some things are real life."

"Like your so-called 'life' in New York?" Willa asked, shaking her head. "So lonely! Nothing but work."

"Come back home, sweetheart," said Maisie, pressing another talisman—this one woven out of silk threads—into her hand. "I could teach you how to make talismans! You have more talent than you know. Stop fighting it. Besides, you know you belong here, in Darling Bay."

"Oh, it just occurred to me!" said Minerva, delight in her eyes. "Our lawyer, Fred Yablonsky, remember him? He wants to retire. You could take over his practice—you would be perfect!"

"What kind of work would a lawyer have in Darling Bay?" asked Addie before she realized she had fallen into the trap of accepting the premise of the question. It didn't matter what kind of work a small-town lawyer might do. She didn't *want* to be a small-town lawyer. Not in this small town, not anywhere.

"Well, Fred had a practice in San Francisco but he has clients here, as well. Wills and trusts, all sorts of things. If he retires, we won't have anyone who understands these things."

"Darling Bay needs you, Addie," said Maisie.

"Dylan needs you," added Minerva.

"*Dylan* has a girlfriend," Addison said. "Vivian Engel. Remember her? She used to torture me in high school?"

"Oh, I don't think so," said Willa.

"She did! She made fun of my glasses, and the way I walked…"

"Oh, yes, I do remember that," Maisie said with a knowing nod. "She had a tough go of it, what with her parents. They weren't around much."

Clara clucked and shook her head.

Maisie continued: "But I have to say that Vivian's turned out to be a very sweet, responsible woman. She's principal of the middle school, now."

"Poor students," Addison muttered.

"No, really, she's lovely. She learned a few songs on the guitar just so she could lead the students in song during assembly."

"I am *so* glad I'm a lawyer."

"Anyway, Vivian's been involved with a lovely man named Ernesto from Point Reyes Station for nearly a year now," said Clara. "I don't think she could possibly be having a fling with Dylan. What do you see, Willa?"

"I don't need Willa's sight to tell me," insisted Addison. "I saw the photographic evidence with my very own, very normal, eyes."

"Oh, *pshaw*," said Minerva, waving away her concerns.

Clara put in: "You're the one who walked away last year, after all, Addie."

"And after he asked you to *marry* him," Willa said.

"Did Dylan tell you that?" Addison demanded.

"Oh no, he's been very discreet," said Minerva. "Irreconcilable differences, I believe is how he put it. He hasn't wanted to talk about it any more than you do."

"I don't understand," said Addison. "Why didn't any of you mention that Dylan's been hanging around Darling Bay all year, making himself at home?"

"You've been rather out of touch, lately, dear," Maisie said softly.

"We thought you needed space," added Clara.

"And anyway, Dylan didn't need to *tell* me a thing," Willa affirmed, a smug look on her face. She tapped on her temple the way she did when she had a vision. "But nonetheless, I *saw* it. It was very romantic."

"Anyway, I did us both a favor," said Addison. "I *had* to walk away. Dylan doesn't...he didn't...he just doesn't fit into my life, that's all."

"Maybe it's your life that needs to change," said Minerva. "Not Dylan."

Addison bit her tongue. The aunties had never made a secret of the fact that they wanted her to move back to Darling Bay. But if she had listened to them in the first place, she never would have left town to go to school, she never would have experienced all she'd experienced. Or she would have come back to stay when her mother got sick, or after law school. She wouldn't have made a life for herself in New York.

But she would have a different life, whispered a voice in her head.

But Addison cherished her life in New York. Or...did she?

She used to. It had been glorious, and so *glamorous*, to experience the museums and the theater, the opera and the symphony, the five-course meals at three-star restaurants. She had loved lingering over elaborate cocktails while chatting with important clients, traveling for work, and interacting with the rich and powerful. Her ambitious side had reveled in the court challenges, savored the arguments in the conference room, and cheered as she steadily moved up the ladder –making more and more money. But as her old college and law school friends started to marry and have children, and even her professional peers started to settle down, to develop personal lives, something inside her had shifted. It was subtle, but something had changed.

And now... Addison hated to admit it, but Darling Bay fit like a favorite old sweater, soft and familiar. There was something so easy, so *right*, about being here.

She had a sudden flash of sitting by the fireplace in Earl's house, with Dylan, and Gustavo at their feet. She had a vision of a child. *Dylan's child. His dreamy eyes. Her hair.*

Her heart skipped a beat, then started to pound.

Addison looked up to find her aunt Willa's hawk-eyes studying her face.

Willa tapped her temple. "Are you having *visions*, Addie, dear?"

"*What*? No, of course not. I'm a lawyer, for heaven's sake."

"In any case," said Minerva, gazing out the window. "You'd best go get that fool man James inside and out of the rain."

Minerva was right. James must be in love with another woman—that was why he couldn't stop checking his phone. Now, standing outside in a downpour, the poor man was trying in vain to keep his phone dry with his coat while he talked.

Addison gave up.

She didn't even care about the farce any more; she certainly didn't have the heart to spend one more night in Siren Song with the wrong man.

"James, how about if I stay at my aunt's house tonight?" she said as she ran out into the rain to coax him back onto the porch. "My back will thank me for it."

"You wouldn't mind?"

"No, of course not. The aunties will love it; I haven't seen them all year. I'll spend the evening with them and just sleep over. Hang on a minute and I'll borrow their car to lead you back to Earl's place and grab my things; I wouldn't want you to get lost in this storm."

Addison went back to join the aunties huddled around the front door.

"Okay if I impose upon you for dinner and a bed tonight?" She asked. "And could I borrow your car so I can go get my things?"

"Of course! Lucy's full of gas and ready to go," said Willa. "I'll get the key."

Their car was a very, very old Chevy Cavalier named

Lucy. It was once black-and-gold, but now sported several large spots of primer gray and red. It wasn't pretty, but it was reliable enough to get the aunties in and out of town once a week for groceries.

When Willa ducked into the kitchen to get the keys, the porch light flickered overhead.

"Oooh, you know what that means," said Maisie, her eyes rolling toward the light fixture and nodding sagely. "Someone is going to fall in love!"

"It *means* the storm took down a power line," Addie said with a grunt. Then, feeling sour, she tried to make amends: "Would you like me to pick something up in town for dinner? Not sure if anything's open, but I could try."

"We have a roast beef and mashed potatoes for tonight," said Willa, handing Addison the car keys. "But you can help with the pfeffernusse after dinner– we need to make extra for Earl's memorial service tomorrow."

"Good then," Addison said. "I'll go get my things from Earl's place, and I have one or two errands to run in town. I have my cell phone; call me if you need anything."

"Oh, I doubt they'll be working," said Minerva. "In a storm like this, they're bound to fail along with the electricity—the antenna on Caswell Lloyd's ranch always goes down in the wind. Be careful, dear."

"I will. And I won't be long," said Addie, turning to go. She hesitated a moment, then looked back at the four elderly women crowding the doorway. "Thank you, all of you, for being there for me. Always. And no matter what."

"No matter what," they chimed at her, in unison.

~

The rain and wind were growing in intensity, but the storm wasn't too bad as Addison led James back into town. He pulled up behind her in front of Earl's house, the windows shining with a warm orange light. It was only three in the afternoon but the skies were dark as dusk.

As Addison packed her things, James looked out the window, into the sodden garden.

"Addison, I'm sorry if the tea reading ruined our fake boyfriend plans," he said. "Honestly, I don't even believe in that sort of thing, but what Minerva was saying..." he trailed off with an odd shrug.

"I understand. The aunties do have a way of pushing people out of their comfort zones." She kept pondering what they had told her, that her life in New York was lonely, and empty, and that she should come back home to Darling Bay. She couldn't stop thinking of the vision she had had, of Dylan and her sitting in front of the fire, Gustavo at their feet, and...a child.

Was that what she wanted? Could Addison have her career, and a family too? Could she change course, after all these years of relentless study and work? Her heart flipped again.

There was no way she was going to make it through to Sunday.

What she needed right now was a hug, a *canine* hug, even if she had to brave the possibility of seeing Dylan. She wanted Gustavo.

"There are candles and flashlights in the drawer here by the door," Addison said to James, declining his offer to help with her bag. "We can check in with each other in the morning, but the aunties say the phones might go down, too, just so you're warned."

"Not exactly a white Christmas, but a stormy one, right?"

"Right."

"Merry Christmas, Addison," he said as she opened the door.

"Merry Christmas, James."

Addison tossed her bag into Lucy's trunk, then returned to knock on Earl's big door.

"Dylan! I want to see my dog!"

But there was no reassuring *woof*. And the voice that yelled *"Come on in! Door's open"* was a woman's.

Addison let herself in. As she passed through the cozy living room, her gaze fell on the rocking chair sitting in front of the huge stone hearth. She couldn't shake the image that she'd had when she was with the aunties.

Could this home really be hers? Did she want it to be?

Addison followed the sound of the voice to the airy kitchen. There were a few dishes in the drying rack, but otherwise it was neat as a pin. A box full of prescription medications on the end of the counter gave silent testimony to Earl's decline. Once again, Addison allowed herself to feel a wave of grief at his loss. The people were the heart of any town, and Earl had been one of the finest, most welcoming, elders of Darling Bay.

"Oh, hey, Addie," said Crystal, coming over to give her a hug. "I heard you were back in town—I take it you got Earl's letter?"

Crystal had been Earl's housekeeper, and as he'd ailed, his caretaker.

"I did, yes. Oh, Crystal," said Addison, returning the hug. "I was so very sorry to hear about Earl. I'm glad he had you with him at the end."

"Thank you," said Crystal. "But he was the one who kept *me* laughing all the time. You know how he was."

"I do."

"And he was very peaceful. It was…a *good* death. Hard, of course, but good. You'll be at the memorial service tomorrow, right? Earl was very intent that I read his last letter in front of everyone, to reveal the identity of the town's new Santa Claus."

"I came to town just for that," Addison said, wondering if there was any way in hell she could get out of it. What if she showed up briefly, then ghosted, simply ducked out without being noticed? No one would really care, would they? Darling Bay was perfectly happy without her, no matter what her aunties claimed.

"Was it awkward seeing Dylan?" Crystal asked, her voice kind.

Addison paused, a hitch in her chest. "Very, but my new…boyfriend was with me."

"Oh!" Crystal peered behind her, as if she were hiding James in her back pocket. "Where's he?"

"Sorry, he's in Siren Song. Um, resting." Addison shook her head. "I was in need of a little doggy company. Is Gustavo around?"

"Actually, he's down at the fire station. Dylan went down to help wrap presents for the kids, and took Gustavo with him."

"Oh," muttered Addison.

She used to do things like that. On Thanksgiving she would help cook dinners at the soup kitchen, and for Christmas she used to choose a family in need and buy them what they needed, and a few toys besides. She had always enjoyed giving in those ways, at least as much as those who received. These days she still gave a chunk of money to charity, but Raquel was right: she didn't make time to volunteer anymore. Because she *had* no time. She had no *life*.

"Okay, maybe I'll go look for him there. By the way, do you know if Sam's in town? I was hoping to get him to open the store. I need a few things."

Crystal shook her head. "He's visiting his sister in Oakland, but he was planning on coming back for the memorial. But now with this weather, I don't know that anyone's going to be able to go in or out of town for a few days."

Addison stifled a sigh. *I should be in the Caribbean right now. In a bikini. Sipping fruity drinks with umbrellas in them.*

"But is there anything I can get you?" Crystal asked. "I think we're about the same size..."

In fact, Crystal was much more petite than Addison would ever be.

"No, thanks, I'll make do. I appreciate it, though. Again, I'm so sorry about Earl. I'll see you tomorrow."

"Great. But at least take an umbrella if you're going to be out in this weather! Earl had quite the collection."

A stand near the front door held half a dozen umbrellas. Addison chose a large black one, thanked Crystal again, and thus protected, headed out into the wind and rain.

The fire station was only a few blocks from Earl's house, so walking would be easier than re-parking the car. Lucy's reverse mode was a little wonky. Besides, Addison could use the walk to clear her head.

So, James-the-boyfriend had other romantic fish to fry in Darling Bay. It figured.

She couldn't even manage to keep the *fake* boyfriend.

Also, Addison couldn't get the image of sitting in front of the hearth with Dylan out of her head; it was a vision of a family. A family of her own. Is that what she wanted? Could the aunties be right? Should she open herself up to the possibility of a different future?

Could Dylan actually be the one, after all?

She thought about the whole-hearted way he used to love her…the way he *still* looked at her, like he did in the café this morning…the way he seemed to understand her, to accept her. Every part of her.

Could he still love her?

By the time Addison arrived at the stationhouse, she was pretty well soaked from the windblown rain. But she didn't care. Dylan used to say she was cute when she looked a little bit scruffy; when she wasn't "so buttoned up and buttoned down."

She was going to talk to him. Addison was going to tell Dylan the truth: that when she lost him, she lost her best friend as well as her lover. That she had been miserable all year. That her future in New York suddenly seemed gray and gloomy and that now —even though it scared the hell out of her—all she could think about was that enchanting image of them as a family in front of Earl's fireplace. It might frighten her, but, she reminded herself: Addison McGee was no coward.

She burst into the fire station through the always-unlocked side door, feeling an excitement in her heart that she thought had been lost to her.

Dylan, Smoke, and half a dozen firefighters sat around a table, surrounded by mounds of boxes and bags and brightly colored rolls of paper, wrapping presents and chatting. Gustavo was sleeping peacefully atop a large pile of discarded paper scraps and opened boxes.

And Vivian Engel, dressed in her sexy Santa's Elf outfit, was leaning over Dylan. Her long blonde hair grazed his forehead. He laughed as he looked up at her.

Addison's smile froze on her face. She was too late. Dylan had moved on. *When would she learn?*

"Addie!" cried Smoke. "I heard you were in town!"

At the sound of Addison's name, Dylan stood up so fast he practically knocked Vivian over, then grabbed her in reflex. As a result, it looked like he was hugging her.

"It's not what it looks like," Dylan blurted out, pushing away from Vivian.

Addison shook her head and managed to say, through stiff lips: "No, honestly, it's fine. I'm only here for Gustavo."

"You're looking gorgeous," Tox Ellis said as he came over to give her a hug.

"I look like a drowned rat, I imagine," Addison said with a humorless chuckle. She returned Tox's hug, sighing as she relaxed into the big man's strong arms.

"Addie—" Dylan tried again.

"I said, it's fine." Addison repeated. "There's nothing

wrong with you being with Vivian, for heaven's sake. I'm the one who screwed everything up."

"Well now, that part's true," said Dylan.

"Wait, what? Vivian?" said Smoke, "I thought you were seeing Ernesto."

"I still am, last I heard," Vivian said with a confused smile.

Addison realized that most activity at the wrapping table had come to a halt. A few of the firefighters still feigned attention to their wrapping, but most were listening in with unabashed interest. The story would be all over town in ten minutes; faster if the phones were still working.

"I'm—I'm so sorry I interrupted you. Really. Merry Christmas, everyone. I'll just take my dog and go. Okay if I take him, Dylan?"

"No."

"What do you mean, 'no'?"

"He's half my dog, remember?"

"I don't mean *take* him, take him. Just out for a walk."

"In this weather?" Vivian said, lifting her eyebrows. The white pom-pom at the end of her red Santa cap bounced as she talked. Addison wanted to feel angry at her, but she couldn't work up the energy.

"Can't take him out without me," Dylan said, coming to stand by Addison. "It's the way canine shared custody works. I'll come along."

"Fine," she said, just wanting to get out of the station. "Let's go, then. Smoke, I'll see you tomorrow?"

"Sure thing, Addie," he gave her a wink. "You hang in there, you hear?"

She nodded. She couldn't manage any words in response.

Addison, Dylan, and Gustavo left the fire station, heading out into the blowing wind and rain.

"Lovely day for a walk," said Dylan, putting his collar up.

Addison managed a slight smile.

"Addie," Dylan said, "You really thought Vivian and I were together? Why?"

"You're all over social media. Photos of you two, together."

He shook his head as they walked past the post office. "I've been teaching her guitar. She wanted to be able to play for the kids at her school."

Addison barely refrained from rolling her eyes.

"And she helped get me a job offer from the school district, as a music teacher."

Addison stopped in her tracks. "Seriously? You really want to settle down and live here, like, all the time?"

"The music teacher gig is part time, but yes. I told you. I like it here."

"And you and Vivian really aren't together?"

"Nope."

"But...we broke up over her."

"We most certainly did *not*," he said as Skip's ice cream truck tinkled past. "We broke up because you think I'm not good enough for you."

Addison scowled. "Is he *really* trying to sell ice cream in this storm?"

"He said the jingle got stuck on, and his other car broke down."

Of course he knew that, blast him. "And I did *not* think you weren't good enough for me. That's ridiculous! It was just that…" she trailed off. Was it true? Was that why she had tried to compartmentalize her attraction to Dylan?

"It was because I don't know which are the trendiest restaurants, and I don't care," said Dylan, a bitter note in his voice, and a bleak look in his beautiful eyes. "Because what most people think is a glamorous life feels like torture to me. Because I want a simple life in a small town…"

"And I want New York."

"Exactly. I think there was a sitcom about this sort of situation, a long time ago."

"Yes, and if I recall, in that situation the woman gave in to the man. As usual."

"I never asked you to give up everything for the country life," said Dylan, sounding exasperated. "I don't know if you remember, but every year or so you used to ponder taking a job in San Francisco. I always thought we could have it all: the advantages of living in the city part of the time, but the mellowness of Darling Bay the rest of the time."

"I look just like my mother," Addison blurted.

"I'm sorry?"

"I just…I look so much like my mother did at my age. And I don't want to live her life, to repeat her mistakes. I'm sorry, Dylan, I know it's hard to understand, but you didn't live my childhood."

"No, I didn't. But whatever happened, Addison, it's in the past. All we have is what's in front of us. And the mistakes we make are our own."

Gustavo sniffed at a telephone pole, unfazed by the tempests brewing around him: the natural one, and the one between Addison and Dylan.

"You know, none of this matters right now. I'm going back to New York, so the whole point is moot. It turns out I can't stay for the memorial service, after all," said Addison, suddenly deciding she couldn't stand another two days in Darling Bay. *She wasn't going to make it through to Sunday.* And if she waited much longer, she might get stuck due to the storm. "I mean, whoever heard of a Christmas Eve memorial service, anyway?"

"You know how he felt about Christmas. Appropriate, I think."

A gust of rain blew under the umbrella and down her neck. "Anyway, I'm leaving."

"Where to?"

"I'm getting an earlier flight out of SFO. I have to get back to New York. I have an important case that just got moved up on the schedule."

"You can't just leave, Addie."

"I don't see where you get off telling me what to do."

"*I'm* not telling you what to do, Mother Nature is. The storm's going to get worse, a lot worse."

"I grew up around here. I know how to handle these roads in the rain." Her ankle wobbled as she traversed carefully through a puddle. "You can have Earl's place, we'll do as you suggested, and you can buy me out over time. We can work out all the details over email."

"What about Gustavo?"

That hurt.

"He's…he'll be better off without me. Can you imagine

Gustavo in my New York City apartment? You stay here, with Gustavo, and make Darling Bay your town. It's a great place." Her voice caught, just a tad, on the last couple of words.

"Addie—" Dylan began, but then stopped himself. Was he going to throw himself at her, *again*? She was choosing New York over him. She had consistently chosen her New York City lifestyle over him. Did he need her to knock him over the head?

"What?" She hesitated, willing him to say something, to say *anything*, that would convince her to stay. With him.

But instead he just shook his head slowly, his eyes bleak.

"I'll just go, then. It was really great to see you, Dylan."

"Good to see you too, Addie."

She nodded, hugged the giant wet dog, handed Dylan the leash without touching his hand or meeting his eyes, and started to walk back to Earl's place to get her car.

"Addie."

She swung around. Had he changed his mind?

After a long moment, he said: "Merry Christmas."

"Merry Christmas," she replied, and died inside.

~

"You, sir, are a damned fool," said Smoke that night as they sat by the fire in Earl's house. Smoke and Dylan and Crystal were sharing a bottle of Earl's favorite brandy while Gustavo snored on the rug.

"I've tried for years to prove myself to Addie," said Dylan, shaking his head. "A man has to have some pride."

"Pride goeth before the fall, or whatever they say," Smoke said.

"I'm not sure that applies in this case, but I appreciate the thought," replied Dylan.

Crystal laughed softly, but didn't say anything.

"Addie and you are meant for each other, Dylan," said Smoke, as he poured all three of them another smidgeon of the fragrant liquor. "How come everyone in town but you can see that?"

"Oh, I don't know about that," Dylan said. "Vivian seems to think we're doomed."

"You just leave Vivian to Ernesto," Crystal piped up, "and focus on Addie."

"Damn shootin'," Smoke said.

Again, Dylan shook his head. "I know you both know and love Addie, but…you don't know her like I do."

"Well now, that's true," said Crystal. "But I have one question for you, Dylan Madison, and only one: do you love her?"

Dylan gazed into the fire, enjoying the sound of Gustavo's soft snoring. *Of course I love Addie. What did they all think?*

It was impossible for Dylan to do anything else. He had loved her from the moment he saw her in that Mission Street bar, and his feelings had only grown over the years. He admired her, he respected her, he adored her. Even this last year, even when he wanted to throttle her, his love for her still grew. She was an amazing, crazy-making woman, and what he wanted most in this world was to create a family with her. But she didn't want a family—and she didn't want *him*. At least, not in the right ways.

Dylan looked up to see that Smoke and Crystal were both watching him.

"It's not as easy as all that," was all he could manage to say.

"It never is," said Crystal.

"All I know," said Smoke, "is that I would give anything to love someone like that. And if I did, I wouldn't be wasting any time."

~

Early the next morning, Addison lay in bed at the Auntie's house, wide-awake, listening as the trees shook and blew, the wind gusts rattling the windowpanes.

New York, was all she could think. She had to get away from Darling Bay. She *had* to. She had to get back to New York, where things made sense and she worked hard and no one asked her why she was doing what she was doing, and no one questioned the meaning of her job or suggested she should be in a small town living another life entirely. No one there had *ever* asked her if she had eaten a proper breakfast. Her head hurt from self-doubt, and that was nothing next to what her heart was feeling.

Fine. She had made her decision.

But when she announced to the aunts she was leaving after breakfast—a long, leisurely breakfast including chocolate crepes and whipped cream—and she asked if she could borrow Lucy to get to SFO, their response was doubtful, at best.

"But you'll miss the memorial service!" said Maisie.

"Oh, and with the *storm*, Addie…" said Minerva.

"I've driven in worse weather than this," Addison responded. In this, she hadn't been lying to Dylan: she had grown up navigating these twisty, winding roads.

"It'll be a miracle if that old Chevy makes it as far as Muir Woods," murmured Clara.

Willa nudged Clara with her elbow. "It'll be fine. You go ahead and take the car, Addie, sweetheart."

Addison gave her aunt a sidelong look. "Are you seeing something?"

"Of course not. And anyways, you've never really believed, have you?"

"That's true, now, Addie, honey," said Maisie. "Can't have it both ways. And at least her tank's full!"

"Well, thank you for the use of the car. I talked to Sam, and he agreed to bring it back from the airport lot. I'll tell him where I park it."

"It's fine, just fine," said Willa. "You go on now, and promise to be careful."

~

*A*ddison had underestimated the ferocity of the storm.

It was fine at first. It took all of Addison's concentration to stay on the road, peering through the sheet of rain on her windshield, negotiating the tight curves of the highway at fifteen or twenty miles an hour at most. But as her aunties had said, she had a full tank of gas. One of Maisie's talismans swung from the rearview mirror, and Addison knew every curve and swoop of the highway. Besides, she was the only idiot on the road.

So everything was fine. The storm kept her mind off of what had just happened: that everything with Dylan had finally, really, truly, come to an end.

But just as she was approaching a fairly straight stretch of road, there was a terrible screeching rumble overhead. This wasn't the storm—it sounded like an earthquake.

Brrrrroooom!

Addison screeched to a halt and listened, her heart pounding.

And there, right in front of her, the mountain came careening down. Addison had never seen a landslide—certainly not twenty feet in front of the windshield of her car. She wasn't right in the path of the deluge, but she feared being crushed if she couldn't get out of the way.

She tried to put Lucy in reverse, but as usual, the car balked.

Dammit! There wasn't enough room to make a U-turn without risking being buried in the mud and slush, the boulders and trees, slipping down off the mountain.

Addison tried again and again to shove the gear shaft into reverse. Over and over, it balked. And then, with a loud BANG, the car stalled altogether.

Addison tried the key again, praying the engine would turn over. *Rrreeen, rrreeen, rrreeen,* complained the engine. Dashboard lights came on, then blinked out. The car was dead.

Addison took a deep breath, then blew it out. Aunt Willa had the eye, and she said it would all be fine. So surely it *would* all be fine. Eventually. Successful New York lawyers didn't just die on the side of a mountain in a land-slide, did they? It was ridiculous even to think of such a thing.

On the other hand…maybe this was retribution for not staying in Darling Bay with Dylan, like she should have. She could have been in his bed last night, if she had played her cards right. Knowing them, they would *still* be there right this moment, snuggling under a warm quilt, listening to the storm, sipping coffee and laughing and loving. Who turned down *that* scenario? Who turned down a man as sweet and sexy as Dylan Madison?

Addison worked with the car for what seemed like a lifetime, but it wouldn't budge. The junky old sedan had given everything she had to give; this was clearly Lucy's very last day, her final hour.

Okay, fine, Addison thought. A little wind and rain wouldn't melt her, right? She was probably ten miles or so from Darling Bay. She could walk back in a few hours, at most. Addison put on every piece of warm clothing she had in her bag—including three wool blazers—tucked her Auntie Maisie's talisman in her pocket, and set out to walk back to Darling Bay.

But that didn't mean she was happy about it.

Addison walked, and walked, and walked. Rain ran down her collar, and soaked through the wool jackets. Her hair was plastered to her head, and rain dripped inces-santly into her eyes. But worse was the wind: bone-chill-ing, mind-rattling, it blew and blew.

An hour passed. Addison began to wonder how long it took for hypothermia to set in. She was shivering so hard her teeth chattered, and though she was still moving, her toes and fingertips felt numb. And then, coming around a hairpin turn in the road, she stopped in her tracks.

Yet another landslide, this one smaller, but still cutting off the highway, trapping her. Could she climb over it, through the mud? Or...if she tried it, would the mountain start to slide again, covering her in mud and debris?

How could she have been so stupid?

And then she heard a sound above the sound of the storm. Was it just her imagination? It was a whiny, engine sound....was that a motorcycle? Could it be? Maybe whoever it was—who was even more stupid than she was, to try to ride a motorcycle in this deluge—could go for help, or even give her a ride.

Out of the gray, fuzzy horizon, came a rider on a motorcycle.

Addison waved her arms, as though this person might pass her by. With the reduced visibility, she couldn't be sure. And as he grew closer, leaving the pavement to start fishtailing through the mud and debris of the landslide, her heart started to pound.

Dylan?

He crossed the landslide, pulled up to her, threw his leg over the bike, set the foot stand, and pulled off his helmet.

"*Addie?*" Dylan looked furious. "*What the hell?*"

Addison was glad it was pouring down rain so he wouldn't be able to tell she had been crying.

"How...? How did you know I needed help?" She had to shout to be heard over the roar of the storm, but it felt good to yell in any case.

"Your aunties called me—all of them, at the same time. They wouldn't let up 'til I promised to come rescue you."

"Now you just listen to me, Dylan Madison: I don't need you to rescue me!"

Dylan looked at the landslide behind him, the rain and the wind blowing the trees around crazily.

"I think you do, Addie," he said, exasperated. "In this one instance, I *really* think you do."

"But not…not overall."

"No," he said, stepping closer, cupping her cheek in his hand. "I'm the one who needs *you* to rescue *me*."

"What are you talking about?"

"Rescue me, Addie. Take me back. Make me an honest man. Despite my tawdry affair with Vivian. Which I didn't have, you know."

She hit him in the shoulder, but without force. He laughed.

"I'm serious, Addie. I know I'm not a high-powered guy, and I'm probably not fancy enough to sit with you at corporate events, but I can make an effort. I clean up good."

"I know you do."

"And I'll never make much money, but I can contribute in other ways."

"I don't want to become my mother," Addie said.

"So don't."

She shook her head, feeling desperate.

"If you'll consider having our babies, I'd love being a stay-at-home dad. But if you really don't want kids, that's fine too—we always have Gustavo. The most important thing is this: I wouldn't walk out on you, Addie. I'm not your father. If you commit to me, I promise you that, here and now. I've seen your good and your bad, your beautiful and your ugly. And I love it all."

"I just don't want to copy her mistakes."

"So don't. Make your own reality. You're a formidable woman, Addison, you are more than capable of making your own life. You've proven that, many times over."

"You should be careful. The aunts say maybe I might be magical."

"All I know is that you've bewitched *me* from the moment I laid eyes on you." He handed her his spare helmet. "Now please, put this on, and climb on the back, and we'll talk more when we're safe and dry."

"You're giving me orders, now?"

He got down on one knee, sinking into the mud with a splat.

"No orders," he said with a shake of his head. "But one very important, extremely overdue question: Woman, will you please, for the love of all that is holy, marry me?"

And for once, Addie said yes.

ABOUT JULIET BLACKWELL

Did you enjoy this story by Juliet Blackwell?
She'd love to hear from you!
https://www.facebook.com/JulietBlackwellAuthor/
https://twitter.com/JulietBlackwell
http://www.julietblackwell.net/

Juliet **Blackwell** is the New York Times bestselling author of *Letters from Paris* and *The Paris Key*. She also writes the Witchcraft Mystery series and the Haunted Home Renovation series. As Hailey Lind, Blackwell wrote the Agatha-nominated Art Lover's Mystery series. A former anthropologist, social worker, and professional artist, Juliet is a California native who has spent time in Mexico, Spain, Cuba, Italy, the Philippines, and France.

JOSIE'S TURN

JOSIE'S TURN

BY SOPHIE LITTLEFIELD

"And one to grow on," Josie Sutter said with a wink and a smile, tucking an extra cookie into the white paper sack before handing it over to Natalie Goldman. The little cherub in the young mother's stroller burbled happily and waved his stuffed tiger in the air.

Natalie laughed and tucked the sack into the storage basket under the stroller. "You've got to stop spoiling Max, Josie. His first word is probably going to be 'cookie.'"

"A little sugar never hurt anyone, did it, Max?" Josie cooed. She'd come around the counter to see how much eleven-month-old Max had grown in the week since their last visit, despite the line of customers waiting. Two of the customers, elderly sisters Sparrow and Birdie Vaughn, were regulars who were as enthralled with Max as she was, and the third—a slick, expensively dressed man in his thirties who she'd never seen before—was checking his phone impatiently. Well, that was his problem; Darling Bay commerce moved at a leisurely pace, and its residents liked it that way.

The man cleared his throat. "Actually," he said, "sugar has been proven to have all kinds of negative effects on children's health, even beyond the obvious threat of obesity."

Five pairs of eyes turned to the stranger at the front of the line. Even Max seemed startled by his statement. Josie's Bakery did a thriving business serving muffins, scones, cookies, pies, and cakes, and while she had added a gluten free line of treats in recent years, there wasn't a single item in the shop that *didn't* contain sugar.

"I'm happy to take your order, but I'm afraid I may not offer anything that will suit you," Josie said sweetly. *Sweetness* was her secret weapon, the thing she was known for, the thing she worked hardest to project. Even when she was feeling upset or angry—*especially* when she was feeling that way—putting a smile on her face and a lilt to her voice always made Josie feel more like herself. "You might want to check the Golden Spike Café—they sell savory quiches and other sugar-free fare."

The man had the decency to redden a bit, at least. "I'm in a bit of a hurry, actually," he mumbled. "I'll take one of those raspberry streusel muffins."

Seeing the disapproving glare that Sparrow Vaughn was shooting him, Josie relented. She couldn't bear for a visitor to leave Darling Bay with a poor impression of her hometown. "Tell you what—it's on me. If you like it—and the sugar doesn't make you sick—you can come back on your next visit and tell me."

She reached into the display case and selected the most perfect muffin, with a trio of plump berries nestled in the buttery streusel and drizzled with precisely the right amount of icing, and placed it carefully into a paper bag.

"I really insist on paying," the man said. "I need a cup of coffee too. A large—the largest you've got."

Without warning, Max reached out a glistening, sticky hand and grabbed the man's pants, bunching the fine woolen fabric in his fist and leaving a streaky smudge. "Smorkff," he said, or something like that—Josie was still learning to speak Max.

"Oh gosh, I'm terribly sorry," Natalie gasped, rolling Max out of the way and digging in the diaper bag that was slung over her arm. "I've got some wipes in here, just give me a second—"

Josie froze, bracing for what was surely coming. A man who dressed like this one, who tapped his toe and looked at his phone and folded his arms and scowled, who generally acted like he was certain he was the most important person in the room, was unlikely to tolerate Max's innocent enthusiasm. She squeezed her eyes shut and waited for the explosion, the threats, the yelling.

"Don't bother," the man said. "I never liked these pants anyway."

Josie opened one eye, and to her surprise, the man was smiling. Well, it was more of a grimace, actually, as though he'd read somewhere about smiling and decided to try it against his better judgment, but at least he wasn't taking his irritation out on Max or Natalie.

Josie grabbed a large cup and filled it to the brim with the steaming, rich coffee she brewed from her own secret blend, and practically shoved it into his hand, while Natalie shot her a grateful smile and beat it out of the shop before Max could create any more trouble.

"Sorry about that," Josie said in a voice that was little more than a whisper. The tension in the wake of Max's jam disaster was almost as bad as if he'd erupted and yelled at her, and she hoped he'd leave quickly so she could serve Sparrow and Birdie and then—just maybe—get a few moments to herself to decompress. "Enjoy with my compliments."

The stranger stared at her as if she'd proposed that he eat a handful of paper napkins. He didn't even bother to argue, but dug in his pocket and tossed a bill on the counter. A *fifty*.

And Josie felt the last of her composure crumple.

"I s-s-said it's free!" she yelped, her heart pounding and a searing pain bisecting her forehead. Everyone looked at her in surprise—everyone but Sparrow, who'd occasionally babysat Josie and her sisters when they were children and had witnessed firsthand what happened when Josie melted down.

The stranger sighed and closed his eyes. When he opened them again, his expression was pained. He picked up the muffin bag and started toward the door. "Fine, mine's free. Use the money to cover the next customers' purchases until it runs out. Pay it forward, or whatever it is they say."

"My goodness!" Birdie said, her stern glare instantly melting. Birdie was a very thrifty sort. "Aren't you kind?"

The stranger paused at the door with his hand on the knob. "I guarantee you're the only female in my acquaintance who thinks so."

The door jingled behind him, the silvery bells that Josie had hung from the knob tingling merrily.

"It's a shame about those trousers," Birdie said. "That was caramel—he'll never get it out of the wool."

"He was certainly handsome, though," Sparrow sighed dreamily. She was a bit of a flirt, even with men half her age.

"I'll have two chocolate croissants and a mocha latte, since he's paying," Birdie said.

~

James Culpepper walked aimlessly down the street, eating the muffin. He'd go check on Addison soon, but she'd been sleeping so soundly when he left Siren Song for a walk that he hadn't had the heart to wake her to tell her where he was going. James had only agreed to pretend to be dating Addison so she could save face during her visit to Darling Bay because he had lost a bet, but he was starting to wonder if it would have been better to spend the holidays hunched down at the end of the seedy bar around the block from his apartment.

His apartment was seedy too, if truth be told. Back when James was still building GreenYo, the shabby one-bedroom had been all he'd needed—a place to catch a few hours sleep when he wasn't coding. Later, after GreenYo had become the top nutrition-tracking app and IPO'ed at a valuation of almost two hundred million dollars, after he'd married the stunning Bloomberg reporter who'd covered his meteoric rise, James had bought the little condo for cash. He told Shawna that he'd renovate it and use it as a corporate apartment, but somehow he'd never gotten around to it, and it was virtually untouched since his struggling startup days.

The muffin was amazing—tender, buttery, the golden cake balanced perfectly by the cinnamon in the streusel and the tart berries. Worth every artery-clogging calorie. James popped the last of it into his mouth with a sense of satisfaction. Shawna would be horrified. In the vows she wrote for their wedding, she'd promised to dwell with him 'in the naturally-sourced, organic, raw and whole goodness of earth's bounty.' She'd convinced James to adopt her rigorous diet and exercise routine, and while he couldn't deny that he was in the best shape of his life, he was also more miserable than he'd ever been…and he was starting to wonder if there was a connection.

Shawna had left him for the producer who'd paved the way for her new prime-time network slot, and the company was sold in the divorce settlement. James didn't miss either of them, and he'd been keeping busy with his personal trainer and a series of women he'd met at the gym, including the most recent, aspiring actress/model Brooke Babson, who'd been hinting heavily that they should spend the holidays in Aruba, until he broke up with her as gently as he could a few weeks ago. Something was missing in James's life—and Brooke hadn't been the answer.

Helping Addison was at least a chance to do some good. James paused to toss the empty fluted muffin cup into a trash can, wiping his hands on the paper sack before tossing it in too. He pried the lid from the coffee cup and cursed when some sloshed out and splashed his jacket. At this rate he was going to ruin his entire wardrobe before he'd even had a chance to squire Addison around town, which wouldn't help her campaign to convince her ex-boyfriend that she'd landed a suave and debonair replacement.

Oh, well. Addison wasn't over Dylan anyway. That much was clear.

It was the emotion in Addison's voice as she'd described Dylan on the drive from San Francisco to Darling Bay yesterday, a combination of sadness and longing that James was certain no ex-wife or ex-girlfriend of his had ever felt, and a pretty clear indication that she was far from over him. It was, he was pretty sure, real love, the hearts-and-flowers kind, the kind he'd given up believing in. If his presence here had a chance of mending whatever was broken between the two of them, then he figured it was his duty to stay.

"Addie's got enough to deal with, losing her old friend Earl," his friend Raquel Verdi said when she'd outlined this harebrained scheme three days ago. "She shouldn't have to deal with Dylan too."

"I don't get how me being there is going to help."

"Trust me—just do what you do best."

"Talk venture capitalists into record-breaking funding rounds?"

"No, dummy," Raquel said, swatting him on the arm. "Stand around looking hot."

"Hey," Raquel's husband Danny objected from the kitchen of their apartment in the Mission district of San Francisco, where he was putting the finishing touches on his five-alarm chili. "I'm right here, you know. Quit drooling over him."

"Don't worry, honey, you know that rich, handsome guys aren't my type," Raquel said, grabbing the hem of her husband's apron and pulling him toward her so she could give his butt a smack.

Raquel and Danny, James' college roommate and best friend, had been trying to cheer him up by inviting him to dinner several times a week and serving him meals his personal trainer would *not* approve of, along with quantities of beer that would probably make the GreenYo app explode. While James appreciated their efforts—and the pizza and wings—he wished everyone would stop thinking he needed cheering up. His divorce had been final for months, and he'd been enjoying certain aspects of Brooke's company, until she'd started to act worrisomely stalkerish. Besides, after selling GreenYo, he'd never have to work again. He had it all—which didn't explain why he'd commandeered the bottle of very expensive tequila he'd brought over yesterday and drank the better part of it himself, resulting in Danny insisting James spend the night on the couch.

"So explain to me one more time what you're making me do?" he asked, as Danny served steaming bowls of chili and giant squares of cornbread. Since the game would be on soon, James had seen little reason to go home and had spent the morning on Raquel and Danny's couch watching cartoons with their daughter Gabriella.

"No one's *making* you do it—you lost a bet," Danny pointed out. "As a man of honor, you're obligated."

"I was drinking!" James protested. "I don't even remember agreeing to play."

"Your exact words were, 'Give me the magic wand and I'll take that freakin' crown right off you.' Also, you threatened to turn over the board if you couldn't be the pink pony." Raquel sniffed. "Not very sportsmanlike, if you ask me, especially since your opponent was only four years old."

James stuffed a huge bite into his mouth to avoid responding. It was beginning to come back to him—somehow, he'd let Gabriella beat him at her Magic Princess game.

"And Gabby said you owed her a real pony, and then Raquel said you could do Addison a little favor instead, and you accepted," Danny said mildly. "Also, technically, it was a tiara, not a crown."

"I instagrammed that picture of you in it," Raquel smirked. "Got a hundred eight likes already."

James swallowed down the greasy mouthful and rolled his eyes. "Shawna's going to *love* that. Only thing worse would be if you posted a picture of me eating this heart attack on a plate."

"Relax, you don't have a corporate image to uphold anymore," Raquel reminded him. "Besides, Shawna's probably forgotten all about you by now. She keeps posting pictures from Vail, with her boyfriend."

"Anyway," Danny said cheerfully, "all you have to do is drive down to Darling Bay and pretend to be Addison's boyfriend for a few days. It's a cute town—Raquel and I spent a weekend there before Gabby was born."

"And this way you don't have to spend Christmas alone," Raquel added.

"I lost a bet to your little charlatan, and it's making me do a little favor, right? This sounds like a huge favor. I was looking *forward* to spending Christmas alone," James grumbled. "After Brooke turned all Fatal Attraction on me, a remote beach in Baja was sounding pretty good."

"But this is better. You can *help* someone. Give some meaning to your insanely wealthy but essentially empty existence."

"I should have just bought Gabs the pony."

Now, here in Darling Bay, he was kicking himself. A pony would have been a small price to pay to get out of this wretched weekend. *Make the ex-boyfriend jealous* had seemed like an easy task, given James' God-given looks and private-school charm—he wasn't bragging, not even to himself, it was just a fact—but that was before his date for the weekend had introduced him to her ex. Dylan Madison had nearly crushed James's hand in his fist, and was probably even now smashing his Lamborghini into bits with a sledge hammer. Not to mention that Addison—who'd been perfectly delightful on the drive up, entertaining him with stories of her childhood visits to Darling Bay—had become preoccupied and distracted the moment they reached the city limits.

Also, Brooke had somehow figured out where he was and was texting threats to come to Darling Bay to "talk things out."

"Excuse me," a voice called. "You there, in the fancy suit. You forgot something."

He turned around to see the angry baker striding down

the street toward him, her mouth set in a grim line. Her hair had escaped its ponytail and cascaded around her face in a virtual explosion of dark corkscrew curls. She'd probably be pretty if she ever stopped scowling.

He waited with his arms folded across his chest. She stopped a few feet away from him, breathing hard from the effort, and thrust his fifty-dollar bill at him.

"It's not a suit," he pointed out. "This is a sport coat. Addison said it's what people wear down here."

The baker's expression grew suspicious. "Who's Addison?"

James sighed. "Long story."

"Try me."

"Seriously? Okay, fine. My best friend's wife's friend needed someone to pretend to be her boyfriend to make her ex-husband jealous or something. I guess she's going to see him at Earl's memorial service, and—"

"Addison *McGee?*" the baker goggled.

"You know her?"

"Everyone knows her. She's been coming here every summer forever. And Dylan wasn't her ex-husband, he was just her boyfriend."

"Jeez. Okay, look, whatever, but you can't tell anyone, okay? I didn't come all the way down here just to have you spill the beans."

"Addison is my *friend,*" the baker said primly. "You're a *stranger,* and not a very nice one."

"What? I am too nice. I am perfectly nice. I liked the muffin, by the way."

"Thank you, but that doesn't make up for the fact that you were acting like it was killing you to wait in line. I'm sure that wherever you come from, you're used to everybody kissing your ass, but around here I'm afraid you're just another out-of-towner. So do me a favor and take your money before I have to…to…"

To James's horror, a fat tear spilled over and splashed onto her cheek.

"Oh, crap," she exclaimed, wiping her eyes.

"Look, I'm sorry, if it means that much to you—I didn't mean to offend you by, uh, paying for baked goods, and—I'm sorry, okay?" James had no idea what he was apologizing for, but he'd had enough of women crying in front of him to last a lifetime. "Look, apparently I have breakfast plans if Addison ever wakes up and texts me, but let me buy you lunch later, okay? It's a compromise."

James was an excellent negotiator—he'd taught a class on negotiations in the Stanford MBA program after GreenYo took off—but this baker was harder to read than most.

"I can't. I have to get back to the shop."

"Then later. I'll come back at four. I saw your hours on the door—you'll be closed." He'd have to make up an excuse for Addison, but surely she wouldn't mind if he took off for a couple of hours.

"I—I have to clean up the shop."

"Do it after. The mess will still be where you left it. Listen…" James decided to go with the truth. "I feel terrible about making you cry. Confused—but still terrible. Let me do one nice thing for someone in this town. Consider it a Christmas miracle."

For a moment the baker gazed up over his shoulder at the steel-blue ocean in the distance. "All right," she said, surprising him. "Make it four-thirty so I can start the dish-washer. And ditch the jacket—you won't need it where we're going."

"Really?" James found himself unaccountably pleased—more pleased than when GreenYo had edged out Lunch-Cruncher to become the top-rated nutrition-tracking app a year and a half ago.

"What, did you want me to say no?"

"No, I—Will you at least tell me your name before you go? I'm James, by the way."

"Josie. Like it says on the door." She gave a small nod and a dazzling smile, one James wished she'd meant for him.

Josie. As he watched her walk away, shoulders squared and head held high, James reflected that he'd learned one thing about his date: she was prouder of her shop than he'd ever been of GreenYo.

~

*W*hy had she said yes?

Josie shoved the door to the enormous dishwasher closed unnecessarily hard. Its motor ground noisily to life, and hot water started filling the chamber.

She wiped down the counter and surveyed the shelves filled with pans, molds, icing bags and mixing bowls. Copper cookie cutters hung from pegs, and racks were filled with trays waiting to go into the two large ovens.

On the stainless work table, eight loaves of pumpkin bread were sliced, wrapped and ready to go. The dough for the pie crusts was chilling in the refrigerator, and a huge tub of Honeycrisp apples waited to be peeled and sliced and mixed with lemon, nutmeg, and a touch of cinnamon.

Josie had sprung into action as soon as she'd gotten Earl's letter. Just like the dear old soul to send her a note that he couldn't deliver in person, being dead and all. Earl was considerate—a real gentleman. She felt herself tearing up again thinking about him.

For the six years since Josie opened her shop, Earl had come in nearly every day for a slice of pumpkin bread or apple pie, and every day he said the same thing. "Josie, girl, nobody makes 'em like you. You must have got this talent from your people." Most people knew better than to ask after her family—her parents were dead and her sisters had all moved away years ago—but somehow, coming from Earl, Josie didn't mind.

His note had read, *Josie, dear girl, I can only hope the angels have learned to make apple pie like yours in heaven. I hope you'll indulge this old fool and make some for my wake, if you have time. With fondest regards, Earl Pickett.*

Earl Pickett! As if there were any other Earls in her life! As if she wouldn't have known it was from him!

What she would have given for a kindly grandpa like Earl, someone to read her stories and push her on the swings, or when she was older, come to her basketball games and cheer even though she was terrible. She had adored her grandmother, who visited all too rarely, and died all too young. Other than Nana, she had only her parents and two much older sisters, all of whom were at each other's throats all day long. Her parents couldn't communicate without yelling, and her sisters seemed cut from the same cloth. They thrived on controversy and disagreement; her parents had sued half the residents of the town. Only Josie suffered silently, longing for the sort of families she saw on television commercials: mothers who tucked their children in at night with a kiss, fathers who played checkers. Sisters who didn't call her names and tell her she was adopted and blame her when they got in trouble.

Josie tore her apron off and tossed it into the laundry hamper and stomped to the tiny bathroom off the kitchen. She kept it meticulously clean and stocked with towels and wonderful gardenia soap from Lynne's Apothecary for customers, but she also kept a little toiletry kit in the cabinet for days when she had plans after work. Being a baker meant that her days started at three in the morning and ended when some people were still eating dinner, but that was all right—Josie was perfectly happy eating her early suppers all by herself, in her blessedly quiet home, in which nobody ever yelled.

Josie squinted at her reflection in the mirror, despairing of improving matters much before James came to pick her up. She should never have said yes! Her hair was completely out of control and her eyebrows needed attention. She'd worn an old pink sweater since her apron covered up the frayed neckline, and her jeans—her favorite —were equally worn, with holes at the knees.

She sighed and dug up a tube of mascara that was nearly dried out, and did her best. A bit of lip gloss, a smidge of blush—no hope for her hair, so she jammed the comb back into the bag without even trying—and at the last minute she gave her sweater a little tug until the top of her camisole peeped out the top. For the briefest of seconds she saw a version of herself that was her own little secret: a girl confident enough to put her best foot forward; a girl who felt pretty enough to have lunch with an attractive stranger (even one with a terrible attitude and a ridiculous wardrobe).

But then the front door jangled and panic hit her square in the chest. She tugged the sweater back up and gave her hair a last frustrated pat. She took a deep breath, and when she walked out of the little bathroom, she was back to being sweet Josie.

James was standing at the counter, reading the hand-lettered signs she'd made to identify the various pastries. But there was something different about him—he had changed clothes. Well, those pants had had to go, obviously —good luck to the dry cleaner who had to deal with that caramel smudge—but he'd put on jeans and a sweatshirt and a ball cap. He carried a black umbrella under his arm. Only his shoes—buttery leather boots that looked like they'd come on a slow boat from Italy—were the same.

"Well, hey," he said, smiling. That smile completed the total transformation. It was though he was an entirely different man. "How's this?" He turned in a slow circle.

The sweatshirt had a faded logo from a bait shop; the jeans were a little big on him, and was that—yes—there was a faded ring on the back pocket from a tobacco can.

"Where's your sport coat?" Josie asked, feeling unaccountably churlish.

"You said dress down," he said a little defensively.

"And you just happened to have those clothes with you? On a weekend when your only objective was to make a woman's boyfriend jealous?"

"Where are we going?" he said, changing the subject.

Josie shook her head. There was something weird about this guy, but instead of triggering her warning bells, she was determined to get to the bottom of it. A mystery! On an afternoon when she should be resting up, given the fact that tomorrow she had to bake eight apple pies before Earl's memorial service, she was setting out on an adventure instead.

"You'll have to drive," she said. "I've only got the van, and its center of gravity is too high. Might not make it."

"You do realize…. never mind."

Josie had pulled on her coat and grabbed the lunch she'd packed off the counter. James was holding the door for her. His manners were polite, almost old-fashioned. And somehow that made Josie feel even more unlike herself.

"No, what? Whatever you were going to say, out with it."

"No. You won't like it."

The door closed behind her, but Josie stood rooted on the sidewalk in the misting rain, her hands on her hips. An odd sensation bloomed inside her—stubbornness mixed with just a hint of flirtation. *Sass,* some might call it. And it felt strange and new and sort of lovely.

The last man she'd dated, a clarinetist from the San Jose symphony, had certainly never provoked such feelings. She'd chosen Len because he was perfectly *safe.* When she'd broken up with him, she'd been terrified he would ask her why, because she couldn't really say…but he'd only told her that he'd miss watching Downton Abby with her and to call if she ever changed her mind.

"Well, I'm not going anywhere until you tell me."

James regarded her with a long, slow smile. "Okay, but I warned you. I was going to say, you do realize that I drive a two hundred thousand dollar automobile."

Josie snorted. "You look like you can afford it. Or at least you did before you changed clothes. And don't worry, the road down is steep but it's paved. Well, mostly, anyway."

James took the lunch bag from her hands, and opened the door of his car. He held out his hand, and she placed hers in his and allowed her to help her in. She sank back in the exquisite leather seat and inhaled deeply. The white delivery van that she drove smelled wonderful too—like cinnamon and brioche and coffee—but this was entirely different.

When James started the car and pulled away from the curb, it purred like a kitten. Josie directed him down Front street, past the town limits, and onto the coast road, but other than telling him when to turn, they didn't speak. The sky was a blue so bright it looked like a can of paint, but clouds were beginning to scud across the water far out at sea. It had rained earlier, a tough squall that had cleared up, and more rain was predicted for tomorrow, which somehow seemed right for the day the town said goodbye to Earl.

"Are you always this quiet?" James finally asked, as they crested the top of the ridge above Stine's Cove.

"Mmm. I guess so. Turn there, and mind the curves."

"This is a one lane road," James said, though he did as directed. "If a car's coming up, we're both heading over that cliff."

"Then I guess you'd better hope there's no one heading up." Josie snuggled lower in the seat and prepared for her favorite moment, the dizzying swoosh in her belly as they descended the steep curves that made it feel like you were headed straight into the sea. Then she surprised herself by telling a secret. "I used to come here with my parents when I was a kid."

"Family picnics? Sand castles and sunscreen, that kind of thing?"

For a second Josie entertained the bittersweet fantasy that Ed and Marla Jenkins had been that kind of parents, and then she let the image fade away. "No, not really. They had a metal detector—they were always convinced they were going to find expensive watches and rings and stuff in the sand. And my sisters were a lot older, so they just lay on their towels working on their tans, and they wouldn't let me bother them."

"Okay, so far it isn't really sounding like much fun, or am I missing something?"

"Oh! Well...the thing is, no one cared what *I* did, so I could explore by myself. I used to find the most beautiful shells, and sometimes smooth pieces of sea glass, and..."

Just then they rounded the final corner, and all of Stine's Cove lay spread out in front of them. The tiny parking lot was empty, just as Josie had hoped, and a few seagulls hopped along the tide's harvest of kelp and seaweed. The rain had stopped, and a tiny bit of sun poked through the clouds.

"What's *that*?" James asked.

Josie grinned, pleased with his reaction. You either loved the folly or you didn't. Her parents had hated it, and in fact had sued the city to have it demolished. Like most of their lawsuits, it fizzled out. "Some people think it's an eyesore."

"Are you kidding? It's fantastic." It was a two-story rotunda, built from ironwork left over from building the rails into Darling Bay at the end of the nineteenth century. There had never been walls – both round rooms were wide open to the salty ocean air. The folly's second story was held up by lace ironwork that reminded her of the pattern of surf as it traced itself along the water's edge. The wind picked up, and a sweet tinkling could be heard over the waves breaking a hundred yards down the sand.

"We have to be careful," Josie cautioned, as they started crossing the sand. "Some of the stairs have rotted through. And I'm not sure that salt water is going to be good for those shoes."

"These?" James stopped and stared at his feet. "To tell you the truth, I've always regretted letting the guy talk me into these. My, uh, last girlfriend was a model, and she knew all these people in fashion…but I'm more of a sweat-shirt guy at heart."

"So you keep those clothes in your trunk or something?"

James reddened. "Um. Actually, I got these from a guy who was taking them to Goodwill after I saw you this morning. All I brought on this trip was stuff I thought would help Addison make her ex jealous, but somehow I didn't think you'd appreciate it. The Goodwill was closed when I got there, though, and this guy was just standing in front with a box of clothes."

"Seriously?"

"And there's nowhere to buy clothes in this town," James continued. "I offered the guy twenty bucks for these, but I guess it won't surprise you to know he told me to pay it forward. It's like this whole damn town got hit by a Hallmark Movie tsunami."

"What did he look like?" Josie asked.

"Old guy, talked a lot about his cat named Anchor."

"That's Gus Treat. I have to say, they look different on you."

"Different good, I hope?"

Before she could stop him, James had taken her hand in his as they came to the sand-dusted steps leading up to the base of the folly.

"Just different," she said stiffly. But she didn't pull her hand away.

~

"This is the best view in town," Josie said, as she shook out the old quilt that she'd brought to sit on. They were on the second floor, up where the piano used to stand, before it crashed through the floor forty years before. Colin McMurtry had been redoing the place, little by little, trying to restore it to the way it had been during the war years, a gathering place for soldiers and their girls to dance with a full view of the sea. "You can get a little higher up on the shore road, but I like this vantage point better—you can see the gulls swooping and diving, and hear the waves crashing."

"I'll agree about the quality of the view," James said, his

eyes fixed on Josie as he helped lay the quilt on the floor. "I think I could watch it all day."

Josie blushed and busied herself with the picnic basket she'd brought. "It's nothing fancy, just *pan de jamon*."

"Pan de *what?*"

"Basically, sausage bread, with olives and raisins. My grandmother used to make it when I was a little girl." Making *pan de jamon* always reminded Josie of how her grandmother used to let her stand on a chair to help at the counter, playing with her own small ball of dough while her grandmother kneaded with her strong hands. When the pan went into the oven, her grandmother always made a little heart from a rope of leftover dough for Josie.

"Is that why you became a baker?" James asked.

Josie shrugged, ready to change the subject, something she generally did whenever the conversation turned to her. Growing up amidst the clamor of her family, she'd learned to keep her head down. Being quiet meant being unnoticed, which was the best alternative especially when her mother was looking for a target for her irritation or her father was looking for someone to blame for his latest disappointment.

But wait. James wasn't trying to pick a fight with her—he genuinely seemed to want to know the answer to his question. And honestly, it was nice to be asked. Josie had been a baker for almost fifteen years—she'd begun by sweeping the floors for pocket money when she was fifteen, back when the shop was owned by the Carpenters.

"Kind of," she said shyly. "My grandmother died when I was twelve. I missed her terribly. A couple of years later, when the local bakery put a help wanted sign in the window, I applied. I said I was seventeen even though I was barely fifteen."

"Did you get in trouble?"

"Not really. My parents didn't care, and when Mrs. Carpenter found out, she said that I must really want to be a baker to lie about my age like that. She said I could work after school as long as I kept my grades up." She smiled at the memory. "She and Mr. Carpenter made me show them my report cards. The one time I got a C, they fired me for six months until I showed them I had all As."

James whistled. "Wow, too bad more parents don't do that. I can't tell you how many people I met in business school who have never been held accountable."

"What made you choose business school?"

"Ah, you know. Didn't know what else to do. I worked in finance after college, and it was just what everyone did —went back for their MBA."

"You must be pretty good at finance," Josie said. "I don't suppose they hand out cars like yours to everyone."

"Oh…" James took a bite of the savory bread. "Hey, this is amazing. You'll have to open a branch up in San Francisco—you'll make a killing."

"No fair!" Josie chided. "I answered your question, so now you have to answer mine!"

James took a sip of the Italian soda that Josie had brought from the shop. "Well, I mean, it's not much of a story. I came up with an idea for an app, ate a lot of pizza and stayed up all night for a couple of years creating it, and then got really, extremely lucky. Skill didn't really have as much to do with it as just being in the right place at the right time."

"What does your app do?"

"It, ummm….well, have you ever heard of GreenYo?"

"Are you kidding? I guess that explains why you were giving me a hard time about sugar earlier."

"So you *have* heard of it."

"Half my friends use it. The other half keep saying they *should* use it."

"Which one are you?"

Funny thing—James looked like he actually dreaded the answer to her question. For a second Josie considered lying to save his feelings, but she'd been trying to give up her old habit of little white lies. Josie had told her first social lie at the age of six, when a boy in her kindergarten class had asked her if she liked the haircut that he'd given himself. From there she'd progressed to complimenting her friends on clothes, asking if they'd lost weight, insisted that she'd *love* to help them move or feed their cats while they were away, and told way too many guys that the problem was her, not them.

The lies she'd told to make other people happy always seemed to leave her feeling resentful.

And it was about time to stop.

"Neither, actually," she said. "I know your app is supposed to help people eat more nutritiously. But from what I can tell, it's just one more thing that keeps people glued to their phones and obsessed with themselves, rather than, you know, engaging with the world around them. Besides, I *like* serving people treats. I don't expect them to eat my baked goods at every meal, but once in a while, I can't see how a cookie or a slice of cake really hurts."

James had been making steady progress on his lunch,

and he held up the crust and examined it. "Yeah," he sighed. "I see your point. Honestly, if I had it to do all over again…"

He popped the last bite into his mouth and wiped his hands on his napkin. "Anyway, sorry, didn't mean to turn the conversation to me."

"No, wait. I swear, you're even worse than me."

"In what way?"

"In, I don't know, avoiding talking about yourself, I guess."

"Okay, I'll make a deal with you. I'll answer, but then I get to ask you some more questions. Okay?"

"Um…." This seemed like dangerous territory, and Josie wasn't sure she wanted to venture there. But it was awfully nice sitting up in the cozy little aerie watching the clouds gathering along the churning waters of the increasingly roiling sea. The hours before and after a really big rainstorm were her favorite, as the air took on the mood of the sea, and the sky took on purplish hues, and she could feel the atmosphere changing in her very bones. "Okay."

"Where was I? Oh, yeah. If I had it to do all over again, I would have gone with the baby pants."

"The *what*?"

"When I decided to start my own business, I came up with this idea one day while I was helping my old man tile the basement. We had these old knee pads he'd found in a box in his workshop, and they kept slipping off, and I thought—what if the pads were actually *part* of the pants? You know, like sewn in? And then I was like, that's stupid, nobody crawls around on the floor often enough to need pads permanently in their pants."

"Except babies," Josie chimed in. "That's kind of brilliant!"

"Glad you think so." James grinned, a toothy, adorable kind of grin that she hadn't seen on him before. "None of the investors I went to did. But the girl I was dating at the time, she was on this crazy diet where she tracked her protein and fiber and some other stuff, and I made her a spreadsheet to keep track of it, and one day when she was obsessing over it on her laptop, it occurred to me—put that sucker on a phone, and, well, the rest is history, as they say."

"Oh," Josie said, some of her good humor slipping away. She'd been exaggerating earlier when she said all her friends used GreenYo. In truth, only the pretty, thin, ones who Josie had always envied used it. Josie herself had never been called skinny; she was more the pleasantly rounded sort. Not the type of woman that James evidently liked to date. "I guess I should probably try it one of these days."

"Are you kidding?" James looked genuinely perplexed. "Between us, I think that would be an incredible waste of time. I was kind of kidding about the baby pants—I just wish I'd done something with my life that, you know, *mattered*."

"You don't think your work matters?"

"I guess it matters to the people who still work there. I sold the company when I got divorced."

"What do you do now?"

James looked down at the quilt, and suddenly became very busy brushing crumbs off it. "Nothing," he mumbled.

"Nothing?"

"Well, I didn't realize it until just now, to be honest.

Somehow, sitting up here with you, it's given me a kind of wakeup call. I've basically just wasted the last six months. I mean, sure, I've given a lot of interviews, especially at the start, and I sit on a few boards, and I've got some good friends who thankfully still put up with me. But—"

"Do you have any idea how many people would give their left arm to be in your shoes?" Josie demanded.

James winced. "Yeah, I know. The car, the clothes, the travel—"

"No, that's not what I mean. You can do anything you want. Anything! I know tons of people who feel hand-cuffed to their jobs, their mortgages, trying to pay for their kids' education and save for retirement."

"Is that how you feel?"

"Well, no, actually. But that's me."

"You're pretty extraordinary," James said. He covered her hand with his own. "Maybe I should hire you. Like a personal coach. You can help me figure out what my next chapter should be."

Josie ignored the sensation of electric warmth that his touch brought, and pulled her hand away. "It doesn't work that way," she said primly.

"Okay. Yeah. I see your point." James shifted so he could look out at the view. "Looks like it's going to rain any minute. Do you mind getting wet?"

"Not at all. Are those boots of yours going to melt or anything?"

"That was kind of a smart-ass remark. Which reminds me, now you have to answer *my* questions. Deal's a deal."

Josie wrinkled her nose. She hadn't missed the way James had changed the subject—or his obvious discomfort at talking about his success. Maybe she was a sucker, but she believed him when he said he wanted to matter. "Do your worst, I guess."

"I'll start with an easy one—why was Earl such a big deal around here? I mean, I'm sure he was a nice guy and all, but according to Addison, the whole town's going to his memorial."

"I guess you had to know him," Josie said. "He just sort of lit up every place he went. He could make you feel special just by talking to you. He used to come in my bakery almost every day, and he always had something nice to say—I remember one time he told me the shop smelled like 'wishes fulfilled.'"

"He was a poet, it sounds like."

"Mmm." The time she remembered best was after her father had passed away. Very few people came to the funeral, but Earl—who'd been sued by her father *twice*—put on his best suit and stood solemnly through the service, then told Josie afterward that she'd done her father as proud as any daughter could. "Just a really nice man. I'm actually making the pies for tomorrow. His favorite was apple."

"That's a really nice way to honor him."

"Are you coming to the service with Addison?"

James stole a look at her, his expression unreadable. "About that...turns out that I've been dismissed."

"You what?"

"After you saw me this morning, I went to lunch with Addison and her aunts. And they, uh, did some stuff and..."

"Tea leaves," Josie said. "The aunts are really gifted."

"Um, okay, if you say so. Anyway, the upshot is that

Addison saw the light and decided she doesn't need a companion this weekend after all."

"She fired you!" Josie crowed. "Good for her. Crystal told me Earl left his house to both of them. His dog, too—have you met Gustavo? I just know Earl wanted them to get back together - he's matchmaking from beyond the grave."

"That's…unsettling."

"No, it's romantic!"

"If you say so."

"What are you still doing here, if Addison doesn't need you anymore?"

James picked at a loose thread in the knee of his jeans. "Well, I didn't want to break your heart by canceling our date."

Josie snorted. "Good one. Don't you have some fancy holiday party you need to get back to in the city? There's probably still time for you to get to Vail, or Barbados or something."

Too late, she saw that James' expression had slipped into bleak territory. "No doubt," he said quietly. "But there's no way I'm going to bother my assistant while she's with her family, and the truth is I think I've forgotten how to book a flight without her. If I go back now, I'll probably spend Christmas eating Chinese Food and playing checkers with the building super."

Josie laughed.

Then she realized he was serious.

"James." Without thinking she cupped his cheek in her hand and tilted his face toward hers, so she could gaze directly into those beautiful, sad brown eyes.

Because she knew how it felt. She'd moved out of the house into a tiny apartment the Carpenters owned the minute she turned eighteen. There had been plenty of holidays she'd spent alone when they went to visit their children and grandchildren. Thank God she'd had the shop— the customers had been her only family during those lonely times.

Poor James didn't even have a job to go to.

"You can help me make pies!" she blurted. And then instantly felt her face flame. What kind of a ridiculous, dumb, inappropriate—

And then James kissed her.

One minute he was looking like he'd just discovered there's no Santa, and then next his lips were on hers. Gently, so gently, no more than an angel kiss—until Josie grabbed his neck and kissed him back.

Oh, *my*! James Culpepper was a heck of a good kisser, and Josie suddenly realized that she'd been *starving* for exactly this. James was stockings stuffed with presents and the twinkly star on top of the tree and the sprinkles on sugar cookies. And when she finally broke the kiss--after she'd somehow ended up right smack in his lap—she felt like pumping her fist and taking a victory lap.

"Thank you," she said happily. "I'm sorry about the pie suggestion, and I know you aren't going to spend Christmas alone." A guy who kissed like that—and looked like *that*—and drove a car like *that*—would never want for company. It had almost been unfair to bring him up to the folly, which brought out the romantic in everyone; as soon as they were back in his fancymobile, he would come to his senses. "And you should probably start heading back to San

Francisco now, because if it rains as hard as they're predicting, it could wash out the roads. But I'm still glad we, uh, you know."

She should probably get off his lap now, but Josie—who had only this morning sworn off putting everyone else's needs first—was going to wait until the absolute last minute, or until he moved her himself.

"What if I still want to make pies?" James asked. "I'll do the scut work—I'll peel the apples or mop the floors or—or whatever you need."

"You…really want to?"

"I don't know what I have to say to convince you. Yes, there are places I could go, I guess. People who'd save me a spot at their table. But I want to be with you."

Josie blinked. "But you don't even know me."

"I know that you care about people, that you make your customers feel special. That you love your work and do it well. That you're a part of this town in a way that I haven't felt like part of something in a very long time. That you taste a little like spice and a little like sugar and that I want —well, I'll keep that part to myself, for now, but I'd really like to spend this holiday with you." A look crossed his face. "Unless, oh shit, you've probably got plans—of course you've got plans. I mean, you're not married or something, are you?"

Josie shook her head. "No husband, no boyfriend, no plans other than the service and the Christmas Day party, but anyone can go to that."

"The Santa thing? Addison said something about that—"

"Earl wrote a letter that's going to be read, naming the

new Santa. He always read a letter to town every Christmas in the saloon, kind of a wishes-for-the-new-year thing. If you're *really* planning to stay…"

"I am."

"Well, then, I guess you'd better take me home. We need to be up by three if we're going to get the pies done and delivered, and I can't do it on no sleep."

"You know, if I just slept over, it would make it all the more convenient for me to pitch in tomorrow—"

"Nice try," Josie giggled. "But there'll be no hanky panky until I get those pies on the buffet. My reputation is at stake—*and* I promised Earl."

Then she held out her hand imperiously, like the princess she'd always longed to be.

James jumped to his feet and offered his hand with a little bow. If he wasn't Prince Charming, he was awfully close.

～

The little cottage was dark when James finally got back. The rain had started coming down in buckets as they ran for the car, and they'd been drenched by the time they got in. Josie's teeth had been chattering, so that required kissing her while the car got warm, and then he drove at about a mile and half per hour so they didn't go off the cliff. He didn't speed up much on the way back to town, so that he could hold Josie's hand, and there was a detour to a lookout point so that they could watch the lightning flashes.

They'd almost gotten dry by the time they got back to

the tiny cottage that Josie had inherited along with the shop from the Carpenters. But then James got soaked all over again when he walked her to the door. She laughed when he said he'd be at the shop at three-thirty, wished him sweet dreams, and gently shut the door.

Now, back at Earl's cottage, he was shivering a little as he tried to fit the key in the lock. God, it was cold. If it wasn't pouring, he'd swear it was almost cold enough for snow, even though it rarely snowed on the California coast.

The porch light had burned out—maybe he could fix that while he was here.

"Dylan?" a voice called, as a figure in a long mackintosh, rain hat and boots stomped into view, water dripping off every inch of him. "That you, bro?"

"No, it's James. Uh, Addison's friend?"

"Oh, hey. Sorry, man, I heard—Addie came by the station."

James finally got the key to turn. "Want to come in? I've had about enough rain for one day."

The man had to duck to pass under the door frame. Inside, he shook off like a Saint Bernard, and pulled off his hat. "I'm Smoke," he said.

"James."

They shook hands. Smoke had a powerful grip. Also, remarkably nice, white teeth. And a face like a movie poster.

"So I don't suppose you know where Dylan and Addie got to?...Nah, scratch that, forget I asked. You're pretty hung up on her, huh?"

"Who? Addison?"

"Yeah, who else would I mean?"

When James didn't answer right away, Smoke's eyebrows shot up.

"Huh. Okay. Well, look, I wonder if you could give them a message. The VFW's just starting to flood, so it's good Earl wanted the bowling alley for the service. Martha's Market didn't get any deliveries today because of the weather, so we don't have flowers. I found a woman who can do a rush job and drive them down tomorrow—she's got a four-wheel drive—but it's going to cost a fortune. Also, I don't think we ordered enough beverages, and nobody thought about ice, and I was going to go see if I can get Adele or Molly Darling to pick up some of the slack—"

"Wait, is this all for Earl's service?"

"Yeah. I thought maybe Dylan and I could figure something out, but—"

"I'll help."

Smoke stared at him. "Uh, that's awfully nice of you, but you never even met Earl, did you? I mean…don't take this the wrong way, but what are you still even doing here?"

James took a deep breath. He could hardly tell the truth —that in a single day he'd discovered that he wanted a lot more out of his life than he realized, and that he'd found the first steps right here in Darling Bay—so he settled for a half-truth.

"A good turn. At least, I'd like to. If you'll give me a chance."

The big man clapped him on the back, nearly sending James crashing into the wall. "Good enough for me. Come on, we'll swing by the fire house and you can trade those clothes for some dry ones."

He gave James' feet a look. "Don't know if we'll be able to do anything about *those*, though. I doubt any of the guys would be caught dead in 'em."

~

At three-thirty on Saturday morning, Josie trudged from the cottage to the bakery in the pouring rain. Her red rubber boots kept her feet warm and toasty, but the rain was starting to slant sideways and had soaked her jeans. She had dry clothes in her backpack to change into for the service, but she was going to have to bake in her wet clothes. The wind whipped droplets under her umbrella and pelted the side of her face. And her hand holding the umbrella was nearly numb from the cold.

Josie couldn't stop smiling.

So maybe it wasn't the most auspicious start to a Christmas Eve, weather-wise, but somehow Josie thought Earl would have appreciated it. Earl had watched countless storms from the snug interior of her shop, sipping coffee and chatting with every customer who came in. Sometimes he regaled them with tales of the Giant Storm of '78—other times it was '72 or '85 or some other year. Sometimes there was hail as big as golf balls, and sometimes it was waves lapping inches from the edge of the boardwalk. Josie liked to think that these weren't fibs so much as creative rearrangement of Earl's memories, and she had a feeling that he was up in heaven even now helping sprinkle the town from a celestial watering can.

Okay, that was probably a little much. Next thing she'd be humming tunes from Disney movies...but gosh, it felt nice to be a little bit in—if not love—very strong like! She'd gone to sleep last night thinking about James's kisses and woken up thinking about apples being peeled by a handsome man in her kitchen. Oh! Maybe he'd take his shirt off once she got the ovens going and the kitchen heated up. Wouldn't that be a nice way to pass the time while the pies baked?

Josie came around the corner to discover that a van was parked in front of her shop. Strike that—*two* vans! One of them had a logo on the side from a liquor store in Bolinas, and the other was decorated with a design of flowers and *Weatherbee Florist* in elaborate script.

Someone had probably scheduled their wedding for today, as unlikely as that seemed. Josie shook her head—she'd baked cakes for Valentine's Day weddings, Thanksgiving weddings, Memorial day weddings—even a green Saint Patrick's Day wedding cake. She hoped that the wedding couple hadn't forgotten to order their cake, because there was no way she'd be able to make them one today—she was going to be much too busy, and she wasn't opening the shop today, anyway.

"Hello?" she called, trying to peer through the darkened windows of the liquor store van.

The passenger door opened and James jumped out, wearing a bright yellow slicker and a big grin. "Good morning, Josie! I'm here and ready to help. Just put a peeler in my hand, and—"

"What are these vans doing here?" She could see a burly man with a gray beard in the driver's seat, flipping through papers on a clipboard.

"Oh, that." James beamed. "I heard that the florist and

the liquor deliveries for Earl's service were held up by the weather, so I did a little digging around and found these guys. Rex here drove all the way from Stinson Beach—took him two hours, but he's got all wheel drive, so—and Nancy Weatherbee had her nieces come and help, and they stayed up all night to get the table arrangements done."

Josie goggled at him. "That must have cost a fortune! I can't even imagine!"

A skinny red-headed man hopped out of the liquor van and approached with a clipboard of his own. "Did you get hold of the guy yet, dude?"

"Er—that's the bad news," James said. "When we showed up at the bowling alley this morning, it was locked up tight, so we came here instead."

His phone rang and he held up a finger. "Just a sec. Hello? Yes? You did? That's fantastic! Yes, they're here now. Okay...be there in ten." He slipped the phone back in his pocket. "Eddie's at the bowling alley now, so I'm going to head over there and help these guys unload, and then I'll be right back to help with pies."

He leaned in and gave her a wet kiss on the cheek. "You look gorgeous, by the way. Back soon!"

Then he clambered back into the cab of the truck and as it drove away, the driver tapped the horn in a jaunty salute.

Josie blew out the breath she was holding. Getting those deliveries made, in the middle of the night, in this weather, on *Christmas Eve*—she couldn't begin to imagine how James had pulled that off. Or, rather, she *could* imagine—and it involved a lot of dollar signs. Not to mention the cost of the flowers and the liquor! Nothing fancy. Earl *hated* fancy! They could have asked Addison's aunts to put together a few mason jars filled with carnations and pine fronds. And all he ever drank was Miller High Life—they could have gotten that from the Golden Spike. There was no way that James would know that—he'd probably ordered an entire van-full of champagne and top shelf liquor. And that would probably hurt Nate and Adele's feelings…

Josie burst into tears.

Not delicate, ladylike ones either. Big, ugly, *angry* tears of frustration. The kind she'd kept stuffed down all those years of her childhood as one hope after another was dashed. All of her parents' criticism and her sisters' snubs had finally lost their power over her when she met the Carpenters, and the town accepted her with open arms. Especially Earl. He'd been there the day she put up the sign with her name on it. He'd never failed to tell her she looked pretty, even—especially—on the days when her hair didn't cooperate and she had frosting all over her apron.

And now his memorial was going to be ruined—turned into some big fancy over-the-top soulless party by the big-city hotshot she'd made the dumb mistake of starting to fall for.

Josie turned on the lights to the kitchen and regarded the bins of shiny, perfect apples, just waiting to be turned into pies—humble ones, with plain pastry and fluted edges, just the way Earl liked them. He wasn't a lattice-crust kind of guy, he didn't go in for "flourishes and frippery," as he called the various toppings and embellishments that adorned some of her other treats. And how were those very ordinary pies going to look next to crystal goblets and towering floral arrangements?

As soon as Josie put down her purse, she picked it up again. She wasn't going to stand for this, no way. Luckily she'd built a margin of error into her schedule today. Those apples were just going to have to wait a bit.

~

It was six blocks to the bowling alley, but Josie made it in half the time it would have usually taken her, because there were no cars on the street, no pedestrians braving the driving rains—and it was barely four o'clock in the morning.

The bowling alley was lit up brightly, however, and Hawk Stokell's truck was parked right in front, next to the delivery vans—Josie pushed the door open and was met with the smell of burnt popcorn and slightly tinny Christmas carols on the speakers.

"Hey, Josie," Hawk said, pushing a dolly holding a towering stack of white plates. "So great James was here to help, huh?"

"Yeah, great," Josie muttered. "Where is he, anyway?"

"Over there, helping set up the bar. Once we get the cloths on the tables, we can set out the centerpieces."

Josie didn't bother to reply, just headed toward the big area where she'd attended countless grade-school birthday parties for her classmates, and—

Josie stopped in tracks.

The "bar" was a long, weathered barn door propped up on a couple of half barrels that looked just like the ones

Earl grew geraniums in. And it was covered, not in champagne glasses and expensive spirits, but...a towering pyramid of Miller Lite, which James was carefully adding cans to. There were galvanized tubs full of ice and more beer and soft drinks, and jars of honey roasted cocktail peanuts and bags of Flamin' Hot Cheetos—Earl's favorites—along with little paper bowls to serve them in.

Darling Bay's favorite (and only) caterer, Lydia St. Clair, was poking at some flowers, pushing her hair back with her other hand. She stood over a miniature half barrel, a replica of the large ones holding up the bar, and it spilled over with ivy and holly and red tulips and white roses and somehow managed to look a lot like Earl's prize garden, both rustic and inviting and just exactly right.

"Hey, gorgeous," James said to Josie, putting the last can on the top of the pyramid. "What are you doing here? I was just about to head back to the bakery."

"This is...how did you know? About the beer, and the roses—and the *barrels*! And the peanuts and Cheetos..."

James pulled her into a hug and kissed her forehead. "People are pretty friendly around here."

"I told him everything he needed to know," Hawk bragged, carrying a centerpiece.

"But the flower arrangements—"

James said, "Hawk came up with those, too. Smoke showed him some photos of Earl's yard from the fourth of July parade last year, and he did the rest. Do you like it?"

There was a note of shy hope in his voice, and Josie realized that her opinion mattered to him. That he'd wanted to get everything just right for *her*. Not to show off, but to *help*. To do something nice for someone else.

"I love it," she said softly. "And now I need you to come back and start peeling."

~

At two-thirty Saturday afternoon, Josie pulled the last batch of pies from the oven. They were perfect—golden brown crust with a bit of glistening filling seeping through the slits she'd cut to let steam escape, redolent with the scent of cinnamon and cloves. She set them on the cooling racks with the other half dozen, and went to wake James.

He'd peeled six dozen apples without complaint, offered to help roll out the crusts, then fallen asleep at the desk where Josie did her paperwork. He'd been up all night, so Josie had let him sleep, stealing glances at him now and then and resisting the urge to kiss that dark stubble along his handsome jaw.

An hour ago, Crystal had called to say that the roads had been closed.

Guess James *had* to stay.

Josie had changed into the black skirt and fuzzy red angora sweater she'd brought to wear to the service, and taken a little time to put on some makeup and tie a red ribbon in her hair. Now, all that was left to do was bring the pies over and help Lydia and Hawk serve the buffet.

She placed a hand on James's shoulder and gave him a little shake. "Wake up, sleepyhead!"

He sat up and stretched, then grabbed her hand and kissed it. "Am I dreaming, or is this heaven? Something smells amazing."

He pulled her into his lap and spun her around in the chair, kissing away her laughter.

"James! I need you to help me load these up in the van. The service is supposed to start in half an hour. And you just wrecked my makeup."

"You don't need it," James said, stealing one last kiss on her neck that sent shivers through her. "You're perfect without it. And what's with this sweater? You can't honestly expect a man to keep his hands off—"

Josie laughed and jumped off his lap. "Later, if you're good."

"Oh, I'm good all right—I'll be very, very good, if it means I get what I want on Christmas morning."

"Pretty convenient how the roads have been closed and you're stuck in town," Josie teased.

"Oh, no kidding? Darn. With any luck, they won't be able to rebuild them until spring."

"They usually open the roads again within a day or two," Josie said lightly, pretending James hadn't just raised her hopes a mile high. San Francisco wasn't that far away… and he did seem to have some extra time on his hands. Maybe their little romance could turn into something more than twenty-four unforgettable hours.

"Funny thing," James said, standing up and stretching. His Darling Bay Fire Department T-shirt—she'd have to find out the story behind *that*—pulled tight across his chest and biceps, and Josie had to force herself to concentrate. "I was talking to Liam Ballard, you know him?"

"Of course."

"Turns out that there's a house coming on the market after the holidays that's only a block from the beach. Just two bedrooms, but apparently there's an enclosed porch that would make a great office."

"I know that house!" Josie gasped. The little gray-sided fisherman's cottage had been empty for several years after the owner died. She'd always loved to walk by and admire the climbing roses over the arbor, the little arched windows looking out over the bay. "It has so much potential, but it needs a ton of work."

"And I need a project." James flexed his ridiculous muscles. "Hawk says he'll help out on weekends if I buy the place."

"That's…wow." That was something to think about later, is what that was. Josie reined in her galloping thoughts, but couldn't quite extinguish the warm bloom of anticipation inside her.

"Okay, let's get this show on the road." James picked up a couple of pies. "Lead on, boss."

~

An hour later, the service was in full swing. At least two hundred people filled the bowling alley, nibbling on Lydia's barbecue wings and looking at the wall of photos of Earl that people had brought to share. Earl had touched seemingly every resident of the town, and everyone from children to old Mrs. Simon in her wheelchair were sharing memories and laughter.

The beer pyramid had gotten a bit smaller as James kept the tubs of ice stocked, and four of the pies were already gone, as well as half of the platters of Christmas cookies that Addison's aunts had brought. Norma was drunk, but that was no surprise—she was always sweet when she was in her cups, though, and Josie thought today she was looking extra-specially twinkly with her blinking strand of Christmas lights strung around her long purple muumuu.

And at least half a dozen people pulled Josie aside to ask if it was true that she'd been making out with a stranger in the parking lot.

Another half dozen women were hovering around James, hoping for an introduction.

"Take over for me for a moment, will you?" Josie asked Lydia, who'd been helping her dish up slices of pie.

"Honey, I've got it, you just go enjoy yourself."

Josie sidled up to James. Addison had brought him a clean shirt and a beautiful tweed jacket from Earl's back cottage, and he was looking downright gorgeous, though Josie kind of preferred him in a T-shirt. She'd have to ask Smoke to let James keep the one he'd loaned him.

"Hi there," she said shyly. "You doing okay?"

"Couldn't be better," James said. "I was wondering—I thought maybe you could show me those photos. Tell me who everyone is."

"That could take all day," Josie said, rolling her eyes.

"I want to know everything about this town," James assured her. Then, taking her hand, he added, "I want to know everything about *you*."

"You might want to be careful," Josie said, nodding at their joined hands. "I guarantee that half the room is watching us right now. Small town gossip is a powerful force."

"I don't care," James said. "Hell, I'm thinking of putting an ad in *Forbes*, let everyone know I'm off the market."

Josie drew a breath, cautioning herself not to read too much into his words. It was just a little holiday fling, two people stranded by weather and fate. Best to simply enjoy it without expectations. Best to—

"Did you hear me, Josie?" James said, putting his hands on her shoulders and turning her so she was looking into his eyes. "I said, I'd like to take you off the market."

"That's not what you said," she replied, a little breathlessly. "You said that *you* were off—"

"I realize I've only known you a couple of short days," James said, speaking fast. "And I know I'm a stranger here. But I feel more at home with you, in this town, than I have in years. I'm not asking you for anything but a chance. And we can figure out the details later. But say you'll date me. Make me your new year's resolution. Give me a chance."

"Well, if it's that important to you…"

"I'm calling that a yes," James said. He picked her up and swung her around, nearly knocking the closest beer bottles off the table. When he set her down and kissed her, Josie was only dimly aware of the applause of the people she loved, who were almost as delighted as she was that it was her turn at last.

ABOUT SOPHIE LITTLEFIELD

Did you enjoy this story by Sophie Littlefield?
She'd love to hear from you!
https://www.facebook.com/Sophie.Littlefield.Author/
https://twitter.com/swlittlefield
http://www.sophielittlefield.com/

Sophie Littlefield grew up in rural Missouri, the middle child of a professor and an artist. She has been writing stories since childhood. After taking a hiatus to raise her children, she sold her first book in 2008, and has since authored over a dozen novels in several genres. Sophie's novels have won Anthony and RT Book Awards and been shortlisted for Edgar, Barry, Crimespree, Macavity, and Goodreads Choice Awards. In addition to women's fiction, she writes the post-apocalyptic AFTERTIME series, the Stella Hardesty and Joe Bashir crime series, and thrillers for young adults. She is a past president of the San

Francisco Romance Writers of America chapter. Sophie makes her home in northern California.

LYDIA'S LETTER

LYDIA'S LETTER

BY RACHAEL HERRON

"I got one?" Lydia held the envelope tentatively as she leaned against the kitchen counter. Sure, her name was on the envelope, but this had to be a mistake. The letters that came addressed to Lydia St. Clair Catering usually held bills. Sometimes—not as often—they held checks. They weren't hand-written the way this envelope was, her name in spidery letters in black ink.

Crystal patted her arm. "You did. Earl adored you."

And Lydia had adored Earl, but who didn't? The man held the whole town together—how were they going to make it without him? Without that smile and barrel laugh, the way he thought the sun rose and set in Darling Bay. Literally. He'd point to the back of Ramsey's water tower in the east and say, "That's where she rises! And over there, she sets over the dock. Did a town ever get so lucky as to have *both* the coming up and the going down?"

Lydia took a second to glance out the sliding glass door. The best thing about having her catering business in the front of her old Craftsman house was that she could look at the ocean from almost every room. Earl's sun sure wasn't visible, not in those clouds.

She moved a pot of stock to the back of the industrial stove and turned the burner to low. "But you didn't mention I had a letter when you asked me to cater the memorial." It had only been yesterday, and the memorial was tomorrow. Lydia was crazed, but of course, she'd said yes.

Crystal cleared her throat. "Yours got stuck at Verlene's. She just gave it back to me this morning. I'm so sorry."

"No, no. I'm just so glad he left me one. You think I should open the letter now?" Lydia felt her nerves race. Last year, Earl had hired her to cater a crab feed, and one of the crabs (off Cortez Burdass's boat, it should be noted) had made the Dunlaps sick. Or at least, that's what they said, but since no one else had gotten sick, and the Dunlaps had each drunk two bottles of wine, Lydia had her doubts. But what if the letter was Earl's way of saying, *You're not good enough?*

"Of course you should! But honey, I gotta skedaddle before the rain really starts."

"Crystal, I'm so sorry." Shoot, it should have been the first thing she said to Earl's beloved caretaker, not the last. Mom's voice played in her head, *Always trying to get things right, always screwing 'em up.* "We all loved him. What are you going to do now?"

Crystal's eyes opened wide. "He left me money."

"He did?"

"So much. Honestly, he left me too much, but I'm not going to complain. It'll mean the retirement someday I never got around to saving for. I'm going to Mexico for a few months. Then I'll be back, and Mrs. Dobney said she wanted a live-in, so I'll do that."

"Mrs. Dobney has eight Pomeranians."

Crystal shrugged. "I love dogs. Okay, hon, I'll see you tomorrow at the bowling alley, okay?"

"Wait." Lydia held up a hand. "The bowling alley?"

"That's where the memorial is. Didn't I tell you that?"

"*What?* Not the VFW?"

Crystal blew out a puff of air. "Ah, crap. Everyone's going to go to the VFW, huh?"

"You haven't told everyone yet?" Lydia couldn't imagine a single place that a chafing dish would look good in that run-down old alley. Crystal was a good caretaker and had been a fine friend to Earl—apparently her skills didn't run to funeral organization.

But whose did?

Crystal looked horrified. "Dang it. I'll go put up a sign at the post office and get Dot Rillo to help me out. Crap!" A quick hug and she was gone.

Lydia opened the sliding glass door and stood on the deck. The ocean below was chopped and gray, and the clouds were rolling in, thicker than the nightly fog and more ominous. The air smelled of salt and seaweed, and in the distance, she could hear the foghorn's signature nine-second blast. For the horn to start up during the day meant it was only going to get darker.

It wasn't fair. Earl was sunshine and light. He should have passed away in summer, surrounded by warmth and sand, not on a dark day during Christmas week.

That said, Christmas had been a special delight for the old man. He was the Darling Bay Santa, and there had never been a jollier one, not anywhere in the world. If only he'd gotten to stick around for another few days. He could have read his annual Christmas letter in the saloon one last time.

Lydia pulled her sweater tighter around herself and slit the envelope with her finger.

Lydia, my darlin',

I don't have much longer left on this earth. Doesn't that sound dramatic? You know me and drama—we've always gotten along, just like you and I have. If you're reading this, I'm gone. Again with the drama! But I have to ask you a favor. Will you cater the memorial? I want it in the bowling alley.

Lydia sighed.

Are you sighing? I know you are. I'm sorry, I know you hate it there, but I loved that place. I can't tell you how many times I whomped Thom Grandy's ass on those lanes or ate Eddie's greasy pizza, the kind that made your belly feel like you were about to give birth to a pepperoni calf. But I love your barbecue wings even better than that terrible pizza—can you do me up a real nice feed? I'll pay top dollar.

Lydia rolled her eyes. As if she'd take Earl's money. She'd told Crystal the same.

But I know you probably won't accept my cash, so in lieu of that, I'm donating a hefty sum to that charity you love, the one where you buy a llama for the village, or the goat for the family, you know the one I mean. And in exchange for me doing that, I expect you to heed my wishes and make sure that there are more teriyaki wings than the honey-mustard ones—those are the ones that always get left behind on the plate. Don't want you to waste your money on those.

He was right. Lydia's recipe for honey-mustard wings

was the best she'd ever tried, but people always passed them over for the teriyaki and the barbecue ones. Bossy son-of-a-bitch. Damn, she'd miss him.

Hey, if you end up using Hawk to do the rental setup, for the extra chairs and things, tell him that I didn't write him a letter because I know he can't read.

Here on the page was a gigantic smiley face. *Just kidding, Hawk's smarter than he lets on. I bet you know that well, my dear. Don't look this gift horse in the mouth, but if you do, get a kiss from that man you've been pining for all these years. Just my two cents, the last time you'll ever get them. Don't spend them all in one place. See you when you get to heaven, sugar, and take your time getting there, okay?*

Of course she'd cater the event. Her feelings would have been crushed if he hadn't wanted her to. She'd make the best wings she'd ever made in her life. There wouldn't be a single honey-mustard one in sight.

But she wouldn't be getting a kiss from Hawk.

And goddammit, Earl, she didn't *pine*.

~

The metal shop's doorbell blared, and Hawk Stokell reluctantly set down his blowtorch. The piece he was working on was commissioned for once, a sea turtle abstract for a rich old lady who'd visited Darling Bay from Marin. *I collect turtles*, she'd said, pressing her fingers into his biceps. *Could you make me a very special sea turtle?* The way she'd pressed his arm and widened her eyes proved to him that she'd been an accomplished flirt all her long life, and he'd enjoyed drawling his yes-ma'am at her, playing the dumb-hick card, and upping his rate to almost double. She'd jumped so fast at the offer he'd wished he'd tripled it.

Fact was, this damn sea turtle would pay the mortgage on his house this month, and if the commission hadn't come in, he wasn't sure what he'd have had to do for the money. He was still paying off Erin's medical bills, three years later. He'd had to use most of his savings just to make sure she was comfortable in her last six months, and even though he'd done most of the caretaking himself, he was broke as hell. The nursing, the prescriptions, her PT, all of it had added up. Would he change a thing? Nope. Not one. Being with her in her last moments, holding her hand as she went, it had been the hardest thing he'd ever had to do. And it was the thing he was most grateful for, too.

The metal-shop bell rang again. "Hold your damn horses!" He pulled off his goggles and gloves. "I'm coming!"

The rain had started—he could hear it on the metal roof as he yanked the door open.

A soggy Lydia St. Clair fell inside. "I walked over—I thought I'd make it before the rain, but holy cats, this is crazy. Do you have any hot cocoa?"

"Huh?" For some reason, the fact that Lydia was wearing a thin white sweater that hadn't done a thing to keep the rain off her body, combined with the fact that she was wearing a hot pink bra underneath, stopped his mouth as effectively as if he'd taken a bite of flux from the torch.

"Cocoa. Didn't I give you some, that Mexican hot chocolate? You still have it?" She walked into the shop kitchen and started opening cabinets. "You got a towel for my hair?"

He jumped. Since when did Lydia St. Clair make him think about the things that involved her removing wet clothes?

Probably since she showed up drenched through, her sweater translucent. He could practically see her goosebumps.

It was a weird feeling. He hadn't thought about her that way since high school (but back then he *had* thought about her that way, a lot).

He grabbed a shop rag from the clean pile. "All I have are these." He threw it at her, and she tossed him back a smile that made his mouth feel weird again. He moved past her and reached into the third cabinet. "Here." He pulled out the chocolate and put water in the electric kettle. "What's up?"

What was up was him.

Super weird. He settled himself one of the barstools that he'd made two years ago, grateful for the cover the bartop gave him.

"I got a letter from Earl. Did you get one?"

"That old man always said he didn't think I could read. He wouldn't send me one." But Hawk's couldn't keep the warmth out of his voice. He'd loved that guy, and he'd cried two days ago when Josie from the bakery had told him he was finally gone. (Alone. He'd cried alone in his truck. Not that he'd admit that to a single soul.)

Lydia laughed. "He said that in the letter. Ah, *crap*, the letter." She reached into the front pocket of her jeans and drew out a bedraggled envelope. "It's soaked."

"Here, you make the cocoa, and I'll see if I can dry that out—"

"No!" Her dark brown eyes went wide. "I mean, I'll do it." She separated the pages and used the shop rag to try to blot them. Behind her, the kettle started to rattle as the water heated.

"You don't want me to read it?"

She smiled, but she still had that odd startled look. "That's not it." She left the rag covering the pages and turned to grab mugs from the open cabinet.

Man, her ass looked good in wet jeans. "Have you gained some weight?"

~

*L*ydia spun. "*Excuse* me?"

Hawk shrugged. "I know that's not what I'm supposed to say, but we've been friends how long? I just think your hips are a little wider, right? It looks good on you."

She was so surprised that fury wouldn't even rise the right way. Instead, a stupid heat spread across her face. "You don't tell a woman she's fatter than she used to be and expect her to thank you."

"One." He lifted one huge finger—the whole man was huge, always had been, even in high school—and said, "You're curvy. Two. Even if you were actually fat, you'd look great."

Was he red, too? What was happening? Sure, Lydia had been nursing a crush on Hawk since they'd dated in high school, but he didn't know that.

No one knew that.

Change the subject. That's all she could do. She flapped

a soggy page in his direction. "I'm catering Earl's memorial, and I need your help. Where did you get this rag? I need a drier one."

"Earl loved your wings."

Surprised, Lydia said, "Did everyone know that?"

Hawk tossed her another clean rag. "When Lydia St. Clair came up in conversation with Earl, so did those wings."

"Well, I can't cater a memorial with just wings. I've got a million things to do in the next twenty-four hours, and I need your help."

Hawk nodded. "Figured." He grabbed a pen and pad off the bar. "How many chairs? How many tables?"

Lydia grimaced. "It's not at the VFW."

"Huh?"

Practically every memorial in town was held at the VFW. It wasn't even something that had to be announced in the paper. If someone died, Darling Bay showed up at 2 o'clock the following Saturday. Mostly they were potlucks, and the long plastic tables groaned under the weight of the cakes and cookies, but Lydia had been hired to cater a couple of them, and she liked the kitchen—it was long and fully stocked.

Darling Bowl was *not* going to have a good kitchen. "It's at the bowling alley."

Hawk just blinked.

She shrugged. "You know he loved it there."

"Yeah, well, we practically lived there in high school."

Lydia's stomach lurched.

Was he kidding? Did he even remember?

Hawk scratched a dark line on the pad and kept his eyes on the paper as a dull red crept up the back of his neck.

She felt a matching color cross her cheeks.

Both of them had lost their virginity behind that bowling alley.

To each other.

~

Hawk's job when he was seventeen had been to clear the low tables of their empty nacho plates and beer bottles. He sprayed anti-fungal chemicals into the shoes when they were returned. He cleaned the bathrooms.

And he flirted with a lot of girls.

None more than Lydia St. Clair, though. They'd been serious for about four months. He'd fallen hard. She, apparently less so, since she'd said no to his invite to the prom, broke up with him, and went with Hank Coffee instead. That was just days after they'd had sex in the parking lot in his 1972 Ford Courier truck, the one that was parked out in front of the metal shop now.

Okay, so it hadn't been the romantic bed and breakfast he'd fantasized about taking her to, but hell, they'd been seventeen, broke, and living with their parents. But it had still been the hottest thing to ever happen to him, and even better, he was in love with her. That night, he'd almost cried, and she'd laughed, cradling his face in the moonlight, covering his face with kisses.

Then she'd broken up with him three days later. He'd apparently been that bad in the sack.

He'd called in sick to the bowling alley for a week and then got fired, which suited him just fine. When he went back to the alley nowadays, it was always with Smoke and Tox, and if his eyes ever strayed to the back streetlight they'd parked under, he'd never admit it.

Now they had to work there together.

He eyebrows drew together. "I don't even know where we'll put the tables."

Lydia tugged on her sweater, trying to move the wet fabric off her body. Her cheeks were bright pink, and he felt himself heat up more, just looking at her.

"I thought by the pay station?"

He shook his head. "Not enough room."

"Can we move that long bench in the front area?"

"Bolted into the floor." In Hawk's mind's eye, just for a second, he saw her as she'd been then: all scrawny and big-eyed, with lips made for kissing.

And she looked even better now. Even though she was scowling at him.

"Well, then where the hell *will* we put the tables? I'm not having my guests eat over those tiny tables that smell like beer, with their sticky tops. Where will we put the chairs for extra people?"

"I don't know—let's go there and check it out now."

She blinked in astonishment. "To the bowling alley? With *you*?"

He shrugged. "If I'm supposed to bring the equipment, we need to figure out where we're going to put it." Going to the bowling alley. With her. Again. Somehow, that thought was more welcome than he thought it would be.

She moved around him, brushing against him. "I need another rag for this. The ink isn't smearing, thank God."

Her clothing was still dripping, but she was worried about the letter. That was just like her.

"I'll get it for you."

"Don't move. I've got it."

In the four seconds it took her to get the rag out of the basket of clean ones, Hawk had turned the wet letter around on the bartop. "So what did Earl say to you?"

"Hey!"

In his peripheral vision, he saw her jump toward him, but it was too late. His own name jumped at him off the page. *Just kidding, Hawk's smarter than he lets on. I bet you know that well, my dear. Don't look this gift horse in the mouth, but if you do, get a kiss from that man you've been pining for all these years.*

She scrabbled at the letter, and it went to pieces in her hands. "Hawk!"

His brain went blank, like an old TV on the fritz. "I didn't see anything."

"You did, too!"

Static played in his mind. *Kiss. Pining.* "You grabbed it too quick."

"You've always been a bad liar." She shoved the torn, still-wet letter into her pocket.

Somehow, Hawk couldn't take his eyes off her mouth—that perfectly round lower lip that he wanted to bite, to nibble—lord, what was happening to him? He needed to find his antennae and tune the channel in clearer. What did Earl's letter mean? "I swear, I didn't see anything but my name." *And the words around it.*

She narrowed her eyes and stared at him, but he thought she bought it. That frown line between her eyes softened. "Okay. Whatever. I only walked down here because you didn't answer my text."

"I never know where my—"

"You never know where your phone is, I know. It's irritating, you know that?"

"Been called worse."

She ran her fingers through her wet hair and then wiped her hand on her jeans. "I'm going home. I have to change. Meet me at the alley in thirty minutes?"

"Yeah. Sure." Since when did Lydia wear perfume? The scent that was coming off her in waves had notes of the ocean and flowers and something even sweeter that was all her. "You smell…um, like something."

She tossed the rag she'd used to dry her hair into the sink. "Are you dating anyone right now?"

Hawk's stomach dropped. "Huh?"

"Because you've just told me that I'm fat and that I stink. I'm just saying—you're not all that, Hawk Stokell."

He'd never thought he was. But for the first time in a long time, he wanted to be.

~

*L*ydia swore to herself as she walked back into the downpour.

Hawk Stokell *was* all that. That was the whole problem.

That and the fact that she hadn't even thought to ask to borrow an umbrella for the walk back home. Well, he should have offered, shouldn't he? What kind of guy was he, anyway?

Okay, he was a good guy.

Maybe a *great* guy. Damn his eyes.

She waved at Norma, who was heading into the Golden Spike saloon. As usual, Norma wore a brightly colored muumuu and long strings of beads around her neck. She held a huge rainbow umbrella with one broken spoke. Norma lifted it up and down and yelled something to Lydia that sounded friendly but wasn't quite audible over the roar of the rain.

"I'll see you at the memorial tomorrow!" Lydia called, but Norma probably couldn't hear her, either.

In another block, she was home (which was also her workplace, but the cooking would wait). Her key stuck in the lock as usual, and her ancient cat Minestrone barely lifted his head in greeting, but that was par for the course for a nineteen-year-old animal who thought playing meant putting his head on the catnip mouse for a nap.

In her bedroom, she drew the drapes that looked out onto Larkin Street and stripped off her clothes. Then she jumped in the shower to warm up—she was chilled to the bone and shivering all over. Darling Bay wasn't supposed to be this cold when it rained, was it? She set the water to the highest temperature her old water heater could handle and tried not to think about the look in Hawk Stokell's eyes when he'd read that line in Earl's letter.

Because, of course, he'd lied to her about it. Hawk was a decent, upstanding man. Maybe the best she'd ever met. He'd seen the line about kissing and pining, and because he was a gentleman, he hadn't told her the truth.

But he'd read it.

And because she couldn't do a thing about that, she'd just have to save face by making herself look spectacular before she met him at the bowling alley.

She pulled on her tightest jeans and her warmest cashmere sweater. It was too bad that her raincoat was one of the ugliest things she'd ever owned, but it had been her granddad's, and his goat Stewball had chewed both front pockets right off over the years. Still watertight, though, and the slight smell of the barn that it carried made Lydia miss him with a sweet, sad ache. Mom had hated that goat.

Mom had hated a lot of things.

Not Hawk Stokell, though. *Such a good guy. What he sees in you is beyond me.*

Lydia had argued, *He likes me. I think he really likes me.*

Mom sneered. *He wants to get in your pants. As soon as he does, he'll be gone.*

Somehow, Lydia had let herself believe her mother was right. She'd run from Hawk, scared of the happiness she'd felt in his arms. Mom said people didn't get happiness just handed to them like that, and who did she think she was?

Nothing. She didn't think she was anyone. Mom had trained her well.

Now, Lydia applied fresh mascara and stared at her reflection, seeing nothing.

Erin, Hawk's wife, had worked at the beauty salon in town, and she'd been the one to show Lydia how to give herself a cat's eye with eyeliner. Funny, though, when Erin had done that thin black line on her eyelid, her hand was steady, unlike Lydia's was now.

Erin. Hawk's wife.

Make that Hawk's *dead* wife.

She'd died three years before from cervical cancer—she and Hawk had thought she was pregnant. *My doctor wants to run more tests, but I haven't had a period in two months, and I just feel weird, you know?*

The weird had been cancer, and nine months later, there hadn't been a baby shower, there had been a funeral.

The skin under Hawk's eyes had been dark, almost black, for a year.

Lydia curled her eyelashes, cursing herself as she did so. Hawk was a friend. Hawk had a dead wife, a woman who'd been Lydia's friend, a woman who'd laughed about the fact that Lydia had dated him in high school.

Erin had never seemed to notice Lydia's blush when the subject came up, or if she had, she'd been too kind to mention it.

Lydia accidentally jabbed the mascara into her eye and swore again. A long streak of black smeared from her inner eye to the bridge of her nose.

She was just making matters worse, and the results were ridiculous. She used makeup remover to get rid of the worst of it, swooped on some pink lip gloss and called it good.

This wasn't a *date* with Hawk, for the love of barbecue sauce. This was a business deal. They'd done business together for years. Hawk was the rental guy. She was the caterer. They'd done so many weddings and funerals and retirement parties over the years that Lydia knew as well as Hawk did how heavy each round table was, how to wobble the speaker dais sideways so the microphone didn't fall off, how to hide the good silverware when Mrs. Chumley was around and use plastic instead.

What the hell was with these butterflies, then? They felt like crows flapping around inside her chest, and her breathing came in quick short bursts. She didn't have *time* for this.

It was just Hawk.

Just Hawk.

She slid on the goat jacket and only let herself regret for a half second that it smelled a little like cheese. Time to smack some sense into herself and act like a grownup.

~

Hawk had gone straight to the alley when Lydia left his workshop, and since she'd said she would be a little while, he'd asked Eddie to let him have a quick solo game. He was the only one playing, and the empty building was a little spooky without the nonstop racket of pins falling and kids laughing. Set up, send the ball flying, followed by a thin clatter of pins falling.

At least he got two strikes in a row.

But with no one to see the pins fall, was it really a strike?

The front door opened. Eddie waved at Lydia before disappearing into the office.

Lydia pushed back the hood of her rain jacket and looked around, greeting Hawk with a smile.

Even from this distance, Hawk could tell she'd done something to her eyes—made them smoky or something.

How could someone wearing a raincoat that made her resemble a puffy, feathered penguin look so sexy?

"Bowling in the morning?" she called.

"The league doesn't come in till eleven. I'm just getting a couple of frames in. Watch!" Hawk lined up his stance, walked briskly and purposefully to the line, and let the ball fly.

Right into the gutter. Even a ten-year-old could have at least hit one pin.

"I'm impressed!" Her voice held a laugh, and he deserved it.

"Yeah, yeah. A pro doesn't brag. I didn't want to make you feel bad."

"What a relief." She'd taken the carpeted steps down to him, shedding her huge, holey jacket as she did. She draped the coat over a chair, letting it drip, and stood with her hands on her hips. She turned in a slow circle while a tinny version of "Jingle Bells" played over the PA.

Hawk tried to pry his gaze away from those hips he'd made the mistake of commenting on earlier.

"This is…" her voice trailed off.

"Seriously awesome? I think I should come in here to bowl at ten in the morning all the time!"

"A nightmare. A sheer and utter nightmare. How could Earl have done this to us?"

Hawk dropped his ball into the rack. "He loved bowling!"

"But this place is so *ugly*."

From a distance, they heard a "Hey" from the office.

"Sorry, Eddie! I didn't mean it!" Lydia yelled. She pulled back her lips in a grimace. "Whoops."

"It is ugly," whispered Hawk. In a more normal voice, he continued, "But we can do something awesome with it."

"Talk to me."

"Okay." Hawk took the two shallow steps back up to the main floor, where people entered and changed their shoes. "Picture this. Lots of white lights and gardenias."

"Too expensive, although I wish we could get a gardenia scent. Does it smell like feet in here?"

Personally, he was getting more of a scent of old beer, but there was a hint of sock in the air, too. "I'll grab some candles."

Her eyebrows rose incrementally. "Really?"

"What? You think just because I rent the tables and silverware that that's all I can do?"

A small smile played across her lips.

Her shiny, tasty-looking lips.

What was *wrong* with him? He cleared his throat. "Leave it to me. I'll make this place look awesome. It's not going to look like a church or even the VFW on a good night, but I can disguise this stuff. Or at least I'll do my best. Magical, I'm telling you." How? How would he pull that off? It was a damn bowling alley, for Pete's sake.

Lydia's smile faded, and she sat on a bench and looked around. "Forget magical. If we can just make it look a little less shabby—sorry, Eddie!—I'll be happy."

Hawk sat next to her. He slung an arm over her shoulders, friendly-like. "You just worry about the food. I'll take care of all this."

To his surprise, Lydia leaned into him. How many times had he hugged her over the years, in the course of living in the same town and sometimes working together? A thousand? More?

Why did this feel so different? A shiver ran through him, and he wanted to take his arm back so that he could figure out exactly why Lydia St. Clair was affecting him like this today, but then she'd notice he was being weird. So he left his arm there, even though he was suddenly overheating. Thank God he'd remembered deodorant.

"Electricity!" she exclaimed.

God, she felt it too. It was like a current running between them—he could feel it zinging through his skin, whapping around inside his chest. "Is that a problem?"

"It could be."

He turned slightly, so that he could look down into her face. Only inches separated them, and in the space of a second, he could be putting his lips on her slightly parted ones. How long had it been since he'd felt this about Lydia? Had his crush on her gone away for a spell, only to come back today? Or had it, as he suspected, been on the back burner, simmering for years? "Yeah?"

"Remember the last huge storm, what, four years ago?"

He blinked. "Huh?"

"We lost power for days. And the roads closed." She stood, his arm falling to the bench. "What if that happens again? Oh, my God, I have to get started *now*. I have this afternoon and tonight to get the bulk of the cooking done. I'll be able to do a little in the morning..."

Hawk nodded hard, trying to appear like he'd been on the same page the whole time. "You can do this in your sleep."

She glanced at him, a grateful look on her face. "You think so?"

He stood, too, but his legs felt wobbly. "You do everything right."

Lydia laughed and put her hand on his arm. That electricity sparked again. The current she couldn't feel. "I guarantee you, I never, *ever* feel that way. Thanks, buddy. I appreciate that so much."

Buddy.

Hawk's heart sank to the sticky carpet. He couldn't think of anything worse for her to call him. His next words came out without thinking. "Want to get a drink with me tonight?"

She frowned. "Why?"

"Because."

"I thought we just went over things. You're going to work some magic somehow, and I'm going back to my kitchen where I'm going to freak the heck out until I have enough food to feed at least two hundred ravenous mourners."

That was so not what he'd meant by *because*. His *because* included things like the fact that he wanted to look into her face for a long time. He wanted to buy her a drink and watch her cheeks get pink, the way they did every time she drank wine. He wanted to listen to her talk smack about how much work she still had to do, and then, when the Friday night band, Dust & Rusty, started playing, he wanted to take her in his arms and sway her across the old dance floor.

But he couldn't say a single word of all that. "I could use a friendly ear, I guess."

Lydia brightened. "Really?"

"Yeah." That much was true, anyway.

"What about?"

"I'll tell you tonight." Would he? He didn't know.

"Give me one hint." She stood sideways so she could nudge her shoulder against his. A bro move.

He didn't think of her as a bro, that was for sure. "Dating."

Her mouth opened once and then closed again. "You want to talk to me about dating?"

Was he imagining it, or did a cloud pass over her face? "I guess."

"Yeah," Lydia said. She chewed briefly on her lower lip, licking off some of the shiny stuff. "Of course. And I definitely have some advice on what not to do. It's been what, three years? You should be getting out there."

Getting out there—that's what everyone said. And he had. He'd been on six dates with a school teacher from down the coast, but they'd stopped, still cordial, nothing between them. He'd almost slept with an out-of-towner last Fourth of July, but when he'd started to enter her hotel room, something had caught in his throat, and he'd been unable to take a full breath.

Hawk had kind of thought that losing Erin had ruined him for everyone.

Looking at Lydia standing in front of him, her cheeks pink, confusion in her eyes, he realized he'd thought wrong. "Yeah. I think you're right. Meet you there at eight?"

~

*L*ydia walked home through the freezing rain and got in her car. She drove to the bigger grocery store on the outskirts of Darling Bay—this kind of stocking up wasn't a job for Martha's Market.

She put bottles of cider vinegar and ketchup into her shopping cart, going through the motions on autopilot.

Did Hawk want to talk about the wide world of dating with her? She had some advice all right.

Don't date Darrel Jones even though he's movie-star hand-some at thirty-four—he'll forget to feed your fish when you're on vacation, and neither Caramel nor Butterscotch will live. Don't date a man who lives in his mother's basement. Don't date a guy who won't look you in the eye. Okay, all she had was about dating men, but they could extrapolate from that, surely.

Maybe, she thought, as she threw three hundred frozen chicken wings into the cart, maybe he'd seek her advice on who to ask out. Maybe they'd discuss the merits of various local single women, and consider which might be his type.

Her mouth went dry. *Nope.*

"Oh! Lydia!" Molly Darling, who owned the Golden Spike Café, touched her elbow. "I heard you're catering the event tomorrow—let me know if there's any way I can help."

"Airlift me out?" It had sounded funny in her head before she spoke the words out loud.

Molly, though, didn't miss a beat. "It's rough, huh? None of us are going to be the same without him. I'll bring a couple platters of quesadillas, and two chocolate cakes, okay?" She gave Lydia a quick, sideways hug, and disappeared into the produce aisle.

God, she was being dumb. High school crushes didn't look good on a thirty-three-year-old.

And the truth was, Hawk Stokell was a great guy. He was kind, and thoughtful, and it didn't hurt that he was hot as hell, with those huge shoulders and deep, dark eyes that always looked like a storm was blowing in.

Great guys weren't all that common. Darling Bay was full of *nice* guys—and Lydia should know. She'd dated half of them, and had been bridesmaid or honorary best man in the weddings of the other half. Sometimes the Venn diagrams overlapped: She'd dated firefighter Coin Keefe but was good friends with Lexie Tindall so she'd been an usher at their wedding. When the music started, she hadn't known which side of the church to sit on so she'd leaned on the back riser, letting the marble cool her overheated skin.

Hawk, though? Great guy.

He deserved someone nice.

As she prepped the wings, she thought about Josie Sutter. She'd been single as long as Lydia had, but just this morning she'd seen her arguing on the street with some out-of-towner. Was she dating him, or could Lydia set her up with Hawk?

Hawk and Josie.

Something twisted low in Lydia's stomach.

She dashed the sauce with extra hot pepper flakes.

There was Ellen Forge, but she had six children, not that it should hold any man back from falling in love with her. It was more the fact that she insisted on bringing all the kids along on whatever date she went on. It was creepy and weird, and even though she said she was dating for the family (which looked to be very true), Lydia still hoped that when Ellen felt like kissing a guy, she'd at least tuck the little ones in first.

Dixie at the bar was known to date an occasional man, and she was wonderful—warm and funny and gorgeous—but the last Lydia had heard, she had a girlfriend, or at least someone she was shacking up with from time to time.

Lydia would just have to think harder. The tiny Darling Bay phone book was still in print—though no one knew why when Google existed—but it would prove helpful later, when she rinsed the chicken brine off her hands. She could skim the white pages for the women she must be forgetting.

She took a moment to pour herself a cup of tea, then put her jacket on and carried the tea out to the porch. She gazed down at the ocean that was roaring and bucking like a wild horse trying to get out of its pen. The wind smashed her lower gate open, then smacked it closed again. Lydia left the tea on the railing and ran down to shut the gate.

"Stupid piece of—" The wind ripped the gate from her and smashed her hand between the post and the latch.

Lydia lost her breath as she froze, her hand cradled in her other one. Pain bloomed purple, first in her hand, then roaring up into her mind. Around her, the wind tore at the trees, her hair, her clothing.

What if this got worse? She looked up at Mr. Hibben's power line, the one that he'd illegally rigged to run out to his back shed, and saw that it was slapping against the acacia tree. What if the line snapped and she was electrocuted? What if the whole acacia came down, smashing her into pieces? Lydia yelped and ran up the bank. It wasn't until she was inside the house holding her rapidly cooling cup of tea that she fully felt the fear ripping through her.

It was silly.

She never got scared from *weather*. She lived alone, and she loved it. Other single friends told her that they prowled their houses late at night, convinced they'd heard serial killer footsteps in their closed-off rooms. They ripped back shower curtains to expose the knife-wielding murderer who, of course, was never there. They complained that if they had a man, if they were married, they wouldn't have those fears, which Lydia had always thought was pretty dumb. She was just as good as any man at handling a crisis.

But now, soaked (again) in her kitchen, her throbbing hand cradled against her chest, she let herself think—just once—about what it would be like to have someone in the house to kiss it better. It wasn't a bad wound. With some ice to ease the swelling and a couple of Advil, she'd be fine in an hour.

She'd be better faster, though, if a man like Hawk kissed her wrist.

Lydia felt her face heat with the surprising thought.

Hawk.

He'd been…funny around her. He'd made her heart beat faster, just by putting his arm around her at the bowling alley.

Ah, well.

The best way to get over that man was to see him date someone else, she knew that from years of experience. And she would get there all the faster if she was the one giving him dating advice.

Lydia put an ice pack on her hand, strapping it on with a large bandage. She put an oversized rubber glove over that, then turned on the local radio station. "Deck the Halls" filled her industrial kitchen as she made another cup of cinnamon tea, just to smell the spice.

And then she got to work on the food for the memorial, because that's what Lydia did.

She worked. No matter how hard it was to forget the way Hawk's perfect, stormy eyes had looked searchingly into hers.

~

The Golden Spike Saloon was packed. Damn it. Hawk should have thought of that before asking her to meet him here. Friday night, with Christmas on Sunday—it was the night when all the people coming back to town went to the bar to meet up with old friends, to shake hands and hug and whomp each other at pool.

In the dim light of the neon beer signs and the one old chandelier that still sparkled overhead, the saloon was one of Hawk's favorite places in the world. Not because of the alcohol—Hawk liked a drink or two on the weekend, but he didn't let it go further than that.

It was the place itself that he loved.

It was great back in the day when Hugh Darling ran the place, but Hawk could admit that since Hugh's niece, Adele Darling, took it over after his death, the place had gotten even cozier. She'd cleared out the cobwebs that used to form whole quilts overhead. There were fancy beers on tap now, and Hawk didn't even give her too much shit about it.

Tonight there was some sparkle going on, too—Adele must have spent a fortune on Christmas lights. A small tree stood next to the jukebox, decorated with popcorn strings and tinsel.

This might be the first Christmas since Erin died that he didn't want to forget the holidays completely.

By the time he made it through the crowd, Dixie had already pulled a pint of Boont for him.

He slid his money across the counter. "Thanks."

"You look fancy." Dixie tipped her curls at the dark blue button-down shirt he wore.

Hawk yanked at the collar. "Too stiff?"

Dixie arched an eyebrow. "Most women don't mind that."

Hawk rolled his eyes. "Come on. I can't remember the last time I wore something that wasn't a T-shirt with holes. Do I look like an asshole?"

"Nope. You look like a guy who's trying to make an impression."

He was. Damn it, he really was. And he might get this completely wrong.

"Who're you looking for?" Dixie gave a half-jump to try to scan over the crowd. From the end of the bar, Norma flapped a hand covered in rings.

"Dixie!" Norma called. "Another salty dog? Don't water it down this time."

"As *if* Adele would water down her booze. She knows that." Dixie nodded at Hawk. "Duty calls. But I'm going to be watching you so I can tease you later, whoever she is."

"Give me a couple of tokens for the jukebox and you can tease me all you want."

"Deal." Dixie's smile was wide and infectious as she slid the tokens across the bar.

He was still grinning as he turned.

And there Lydia was, right there in front of him. All five foot three of her, Lydia St. Clair, looking like the day they graduated from high school—those twinkly blue eyes, that slightly suspicious smile…and was she…

Was she wearing the same clothes as she had back then?

She didn't look *bad*. Hell, no. He didn't think she could.

But she was tugging off a ripped black hoodie, and under that she wore an INXS T-shirt that he could swear she'd owned back then. He'd sat behind her in math, and there had been a rip at the back of the neck.

"Excuse me." Hawk put his hands on her shoulders.

"What?"

He turned her slowly. Yep, there was the rip. A little bigger, now it showed a flash of her red bra-strap, and suddenly Hawk thanked the heavens that Lydia St. Clair was thrifty that way. Holy crap, if she'd been flashing that bra in math, he never would have passed algebra. Alge*BRA*.

She spun back to face him. "First, what was that? And second, why are you laughing?"

"Nothing. I was just checking something."

"My ass?"

"Damnit. I forgot to check that while I was looking." It was the truth, and it slipped out. He saw a corner of her mouth quirk as if she was battling a smile.

"Get me a beer?" Lydia pointed. "I'll grab that table. Then you can tell me your woes."

His woes? Why did she say that?

Dixie was back from serving Norma. "You're on a date with *Lydia*?"

He nodded. "Can I get another Boont for her, please?"

Dixie pulled the draft and slid it to him. "On the house. This I gotta see. She didn't get the dressing-up memo, I see."

"Huh?" Should he be embarrassed by what he was wearing? It wasn't like he was in a damn suit—it was just a button-down with his good jeans.

She shook her head. "That woman has been in love with you forever. Are you the only one blind to that?" She swatted her hands with a broom gesture. "Go. Git. Sit where I can see you."

He would not. At the table with Lydia, he deliberately angled his chair so that he was hidden from Dixie's view by Parrot Freddy's breadth.

Lydia?

In love with him?

"Your beer." He handed it to her. When their fingers met, he was reminded of the time he fell off a log while crossing Lathrop Creek—same jolt, the same sense of falling.

"Thanks," she said, apparently unaffected.

Same splash.

"How did prep go?"

"Oh, fine." She lifted a bruised, swollen hand. "Smashed my hand in the gate, but all the fingers work."

"What?" Without thinking, he scooted his chair so that it was next to hers. He took her forearm gently in his, lifting it like it was a hot piece of iron ore that might suddenly twist the wrong way. "This looks awful. Did you go to the doctor?"

"Nah. I promise, nothing's broken."

He moved his fingers as gently as possible. "Tell me if I hurt you at all."

~

He traced his thumb over the worst of the bruise on the back of her hand, a whisper of touch, so soft she could barely feel it.

Lydia sucked in a breath.

He froze. "Did that hurt?"

The whole hand ached, and it would, until it had healed. Till then, she'd just keep using it, if gingerly so. "You're like me —we don't get days off because we feel bad. I can suck it up."

Hawk looked up at her, and for one long second, his gaze tangled in hers. She forgot what they were there to do —if asked, she might not have been able to remember her own name without a moment's warning.

All she could see were those dark eyes, hawk-like in their intensity. Something dropped in her stomach, and she swayed. "I'm fine—"

He kissed her hand.

The back of it.

Like she was the queen or something.

His lips stayed there, warm on the bruise, making her hand throb even harder, though somehow the pain was gone, leaving nothing behind but a faint buzzing in the front of her mind.

"Oh," she said.

His fingers played along the line of her wrist, stroking her palm, while he kept his soft lips on the back of her hand. Lydia was vaguely conscious of the eyes of the bar taking in this very out-of-the-ordinary meeting between two platonic friends.

None of this felt platonic. Not the soft sweep of his lips, and definitely not the touch of his fingertips on her wrist. *Definitely* not that long eye-lock, the kind that felt like the look you give someone right before you both agree that sex is on the menu that night.

Confusion swelled in Lydia's chest, robbing her of breath. She yanked her hand away, gasping.

She'd blame that stupid gasp on the pain, which was back.

Hawk looked cool, though, like there was nothing the slightest bit weird about him kissing her owie. "You sure I can't take you to the doc in the box? Get that X-rayed? I don't mind driving you."

She gestured toward the doors. "In that mess? It's coming down even worse now. They say the main road is going to go soon. I even heard someone say we might get snow, can you imagine? I'm not going out in that for a silly hand that's not broken." She shifted in her seat. Her jeans, which had fit at home, suddenly felt too tight. Her favorite T-shirt felt too thin—had he seen the tear in the back? Why had he turned her around?

Was it her fate to just keep feeling turned around tonight? "Okay, let's get down to business."

His eyebrows jumped, but his smile stayed. When had those fine lines crept to the corners of his eyes? Somehow he looked even more handsome with them—they matched the laugh lines at the edges of his lips.

Those lips.

"Um…"

Hawk said, "Business?"

"I'm supposed to be helping you, right?"

"Yeah. That's right. I guess."

Lydia was *so* confused. "I'm sorry. I thought you wanted dating advice."

"I did. But I don't anymore. I kind of just want to date you."

She used her good hand to hold the beer bottle and took two long swallows. The Boont burned her throat, and bubbles rose in her throat. Or was that her soul?

"Come on, Hawk." He was good at practical jokes. In high school, he'd put a cow on top of the wood shop. Once he'd convinced Mandy Keeler that he was a spy. In the middle of his and Erin's wedding, he'd had his cousin pull the fire alarm, so they had to troop out of the wedding to see the skywriter he'd hired to write *This is your last chance to back out!*

Tonight's practical joke didn't feel very funny, though. "Date me. Date *me*?"

"Yeah." He pressed his palms to the top of the small table. Was it possible that he was nervous, too? "I don't know why it's never occurred to me before."

Oh, my God, could he have possibly forgotten…

He went on, "I've always just had you in the friend category in my mind."

Lydia narrowed her eyes. "Always?" What about that time in his pickup truck?

"Well. Almost always." The fire that leaped in his eyes said he *did* remember the truck.

Lydia fiddled with the paper on the bottle. "That was a long time ago. We were kids."

He looked relieved. "Yeah. Kids. Kids do dumb things, don't they? But hey. What if we tried it? Dating? You and me?"

It wasn't sorrow, really, that folded around her organs, but it was something like it—a thick disappointment.

They were the words she'd imagined hearing a million times since she'd broken up with him after they'd had sex that one time, her first time.

But she'd imagined it so differently. In all her 2 a.m. ridiculous yearnings, he'd come to her and said, "I never got over you. You've always been the one. Why did you break up with me back then? I've needed you ever since."

She'd broken up with him because she'd been scared—it was too intense, and she hadn't felt ready for it, for him, for more, for something that might actually turn into true love. She'd only been seventeen.

But she'd forgotten to tell him that was why. The kids called it ghosting now. Josie said it was looked down on. *You don't just leave someone hanging. That's cold.*

It was what she'd done, though.

And up till this very moment, sitting on the edge of the very crowded saloon, she realized that what she'd wanted was for him to chase her. To come find her and tell her that he'd been waiting for her ever since.

But he hadn't. He'd moved on, like a normal person. Really, so had she. She'd had good boyfriends and bad ones. She'd fallen in lust a lot, and in love twice, though neither time stuck.

Always, though, she'd let herself occasionally dream of the moment that Hawk Stokell came and pounded on her front door, yelling, "It's always been you! It's been you all along."

And now that he was into the idea of maybe dating a little bit? What was it he'd said? *I kind of just want to date you.*

Lydia took another sip of her beer without meeting his eyes. It tasted sour.

She wasn't going to recover if she fell again. When she was younger, she bounced. Now, she felt like she might break. "No offense, Hawk, but I think—"

He stood, taking her good hand. "Dance with me?"

Dust & Rusty were just taking the stage. Nate was at the front, his cowboy hat tipped back. His wife Adele looked like she was going to sing this set with them, which meant that they'd open with something slow, a love song or a waltz.

Lydia had to get out of here—so why were her feet following him onto the floor? She was a grown-ass woman, and she knew exactly how to say that she didn't want something.

It's just that she *did* want this.

Could you get a refund on a wasted heart? One that had spent years stupidly yearning? She took a deep breath as Hawk pulled her into his arms, and decided, once she was pulled into them, confronted with the way he smelled, of soap and iron and something spicy, that even if she could get a refund, she wouldn't ask for one.

This might be guaranteed to hurt her, but just like the hand she could barely feel right now, pain was temporary.

Run, she told herself. *Run. I'm not good enough for you.*

Then she let him pull her even closer.

The song was slow—the way Dust & Rusty liked to open. Instead of stirring up the bar with a great whoop, they eased in gradually. The song was bluesy and sad, and Lydia realized that the feeling of Hawk's hand pressing on the small of her back was possibly the best thing she'd felt in years.

Then she thought about other things she might be able to feel with him if they were…dating.

A whisper grazed her temple. Had he said something? Even with the slow song, it was loud in here. "What?" she said.

His eyes caught hers again, and her knees went white-hot. "Didn't say nothin'."

Dating would be the worst. They'd go out to dinners, and they'd see movies, and eventually, he'd want to break up with her so he could fall in love with someone as awesome and nice as Erin had been (not that Lydia wasn't nice—she knew she was—she just wasn't *perfect* like Erin had been) and then her heart would get broken. Was the sex worth all that?

Yes, yes it would be, said her body.

I can't bear it again, said her heart.

You're a traitorous idiot, said her brain.

She raised her lips to his ear. "I'm sorry. This isn't a good idea. I'll see you tomorrow at set up, okay? Early. Really early."

And she ran.

It wasn't until she was running home through the dark that she realized the rain had briefly paused and her tears were frozen on her cheeks.

~

*H*awk barely slept.

It wasn't the rain that sounded like artillery on the roof, though he wanted to blame it on that.

She'd run.

Again.

Just like back then. *Damn,* he'd had such a thing for Lydia back in the day, and it was worse now than it had ever been at its height. How had he not seen this coming? The crush—god, it felt like more than that—had landed on him like a ton of bricks, fully formed, as if he'd never gotten over her.

Lydia was the same as she was back then, only better. The way she'd felt in his arms—it was different. Back then, he'd trembled when he'd kissed her. The fact that they'd lost their virginity to each other? That had made it special. But while they were dancing, he'd felt the weight of the years that had passed. They were different now. They'd seen tragedy and loss, and happiness and joy. They weren't kids.

But this time, he hadn't even so much as kissed her, and she'd still run out of his arms.

What the *hell* was he doing wrong?

A giant gust of wind blew into the side of the house, and the roof creaked under the weight of water dumping onto it.

And was that...dripping? He rolled out of bed with a groan and padded to the kitchen. Yep, there it was, a leak sending water to the floor next to the stove. Fantastic. The storm was supposed to last for the next two days, maybe more. He put the biggest pot he owned beneath the torrent and hoped it would be enough. If it wasn't? Well, he had a lot of shop rags lying around.

Lydia's face flashed in front of his eyes. Those lips of hers—what if he'd kissed her on the dance floor? Nah, that would have made it even worse. Was it possible that the attraction was only one way, from his side? He hadn't thought so, but good grief, when a woman fled a date that had only lasted less than an hour, he must be the worst date in the entire universe.

He started a pot of coffee—there'd be no more sleep tonight. Maybe he could get some work on the sea turtle done before starting to load tables and chairs into the bowling alley at eight.

He glanced at his phone for the time—three-thirty in the morning. As he set it down on the counter, it buzzed with a text.

Lydia.

What if she was texting? He scrambled to grab the phone so fast that he dropped it. *Come on, Stokell.*

But it wasn't her. It was from Crystal, of all people.

Code red! Can you get to the bowling alley? Some guy from San Francisco managed to get a couple of trucks to drive through the rain with supplies—need help carting it in.

He typed back, *It's the middle of the night, Crystal.*

I know, and I'm sorry. But the trucks have to get back out fast, in case the roads close.

He sighed but felt a tinge of relief. He wouldn't have to mope around for hours—he could get the job done at the alley and then come home for a nap before the service.

Hawk plunged out into the rain, cursing the downpour as he ran to his truck. The rain was going to make it miserable to load in, but at least it was a distraction.

From her.

The guy who'd gotten the alcohol and flowers through the storm was named James, and he seemed like a person Hawk would have liked if he were in the mood to like anyone. For a city guy who didn't know Earl, he sure seemed to have gotten the memo on what Earl would have asked for at his memorial. Instead of fancy beer, there were stacks of Miller Lite. James had brought in wine barrels full of blooming geraniums, and extra full-sized barrels that stood around as tables.

"Hey, guy, thanks." Hawk stuck out his hand. "I'm only gonna need to bring in half my stuff, and that's awesome…" His voice trailed off as he saw Lydia carry in a bouquet.

She was drenched even with her massive old coat on, and she looked like she was freezing—her cheeks were white.

And she went whiter as she looked at him.

James was saying something to him, but he couldn't hear him through the rush of blood in his ears.

"Sorry. Excuse me." He crossed the room toward her.

Her face got even paler. "I'm sorry," she said.

What was she sorry for? Breaking his heart those many years ago? Breaking it again just hours ago on the dance floor? "What did I do wrong?"

Lydia shook her head. "Nothing. I've always been the problem."

W̃hat had he *done*? Besides being perfect—in looks, in manner, in sexiness, in rugged appeal, in just about everything?

He had her heart.

And she really wanted it back.

It wasn't *safe* to want him. Years ago, her mother had made it clear—he was way out of her league. When he'd married Erin, Mom had been proven right. Erin had been so perfect Lydia hadn't even been jealous. It had just been obvious. Of course he'd choose a woman like her.

And he'd do it again, leaving her alone, like Mom always said she deserved to be. Mom was always kind of miserable, but she was smart, and she'd been right about so much (Dad's leaving them, Granddad's cancer, all of it). She'd probably been right about that, too.

Lydia looked up at him—the sheer mass of him made her want to lean forward into him, letting him catch her. But she stayed still. She didn't sway. "I'm not good for you."

From the direction of the pile of Flamin' Hot Cheetos came a crashing noise. Someone cursed and then there was a tinkle of broken glass.

Hawk smiled. "Oh, come on, Lydia."

But she didn't let herself smile back.

His bright look faded like worn denim. "You're serious."

Lydia clenched her fists so hard her nails bit into her palms. "I just can't get hurt again."

"Again." His voice was flat.

Josie bustled past, her arms full of pies. "I'm usually all by myself at this time of the morning. Isn't this place looking great?"

Lydia pasted on a grimace. "Sure is."

Hawk's eyes didn't leave her face. She could almost feel his gaze, as if he were reaching out to touch her, but his hands stayed in his pockets.

Lydia wanted to just tell him the *truth.* What if she did? What if she confessed how she'd felt about him her entire life? She felt too tired to keep up the façade anymore. She didn't look at him as just a friend, never had. She'd never fit into his life, and she had to get over him. Keeping it secret from him had been the easiest way to try to get over him, up till now. Now it wasn't working.

"What is it?" He stepped closer, and his voice was so low she could feel its rumble. "Tell me."

There had to be a private place they could go to, to get out of this insane early-morning crowd. Lydia waved a hand. "I can't—not here—"

"The back office. Come on." Hawk took her hand and led her.

God help her, she followed, her hand swallowed by his —she could feel every callus, every rough spot he'd earned from the heat of his metalwork. Her fingers twined with his so naturally, like they'd always been there. Lydia could almost hear her heart split into tiny fragments like the glass that had shattered a minute before.

Hawk stopped short, and Lydia almost ran into him. "Crap," he said.

Eddie filled the office. He spilled out of his office chair, his feet up on his desk. He snored triumphantly.

She tried to tug her hand back. "It's fine. It's nothing."

"No, we have to talk. C'mon. Follow me, darlin'."

Darlin'.

She'd follow him anywhere. That was her whole problem.

Hawk led her back through the bowling alley. James stood on a ladder stringing white lights from every available surface. Josie and Crystal were straightening tablecloths and setting out candles, still unlit. They didn't even seem to notice that Hawk was holding her hand though she could have sworn their clasped palms lit up like streetlights.

"Where are we—?"

"Do you trust me?" Hawk paused at the front glass door as he shrugged off his coat.

He let go of her hand to do so, and her whole body felt colder without his warmth.

"I trust you." She did, somehow. She always would.

He threw open the door, and a frigid, wet gust knocked into them. Tossing his coat over her, he tucked her under his arm. Together, they ran to his truck. By the time she was inside the cab and he was around to his side, he was soaked to the skin. Lydia had barely felt a drop.

"There," he gasped. He started the truck and turned on the heater. "We're going to have to be environmentally irresponsible for a minute. Got to get you warmed up."

It's true, she was shivering, but not from cold. Lydia felt heat in her core radiating to her skin—she was terrified.

So it was better to get it over with. "I'm in love with you." *Oh, Jesus on a postage stamp, where did that come from?*

Hawk had been slicking the rain from his face. He stopped, his hand still covering his stubbled jaw. "Sorry?"

"Oh, my god, I didn't even *know* that until one second ago."

"When you said it." His hand fell, but he remained completely still otherwise. "You realized it. Then?"

Good lord, what was she doing? "That's not what I was going to tell you! That's not my secret!"

He kept his voice low as if he didn't want to startle her. "Well, what was the *actual* secret?"

"I thought it was that I hadn't gotten over you in high school." Yep. Here it came. The words swam up her throat, and there, in the heated cab that smelled like wool and metal, in the very place she'd made love with him exactly once in her life, all the words tumbled out. "I *thought* my secret was that I thought I wasn't good enough for you, and I know, I know—I'm a modern woman and I'm a feminist, but I still thought you were too good for me, and then when we became such good friends, I thought that I could handle it, and I've worked with you now for years and years, and I miss you when I don't see you, and you're the first person I think of when I wake up and the last person I think of at night—" Oh, no, she would have to plead a stroke or something else serious to get her out of this later, but right now she couldn't stop herself. "I didn't even know I was in love with you till, um, like I said, this second, but don't worry." She patted his hand and felt more ridiculous than she ever had in her whole life. "I'll get over you, starting tomorrow. Promise."

His mouth fell open as if weighted. "You thought I was too *good* for you?"

Lydia blinked back a sudden heat at the back of her eyes and shrugged.

He went on, "Then why the hell did you break up with me in high school?"

"That." She nodded. "What you just said."

"But I was a kid. So were you. How could either of us have been too good or bad for each other?"

"Yeah, well." She regretted every word now. She'd go home and get in bed and lie down and die, and her ancient cat Minestrone would die, too, because he wouldn't eat her because he didn't have any teeth, but at least she wasn't shortening his life too tragically.

"Your *mom* said that." He shifted in his seat so that he was facing her. His chambray shirt still dripped, and his eyes blazed.

"She did, but I knew it was—"

"She was wrong. You know that."

Technically, Lydia knew it. She was a solid citizen. She paid her taxes and her mortgage on time. She'd run her own business for five years without once getting sued.

But it didn't change the voice in her head. *If I'd known I'd get you, I'd never have had you. The abortion was too expensive. That was my whole problem.*

"Your mom was a bitch."

Lydia sucked in a breath. "Excuse me?"

"Straight up. You know the whole town hated her, right?"

"Hawk Stokell!" It was one thing to dislike your own mother; it was a whole other thing to hear someone say it (and to feel this sudden, odd thrill because of it).

"She was a nasty piece of work. You know she once called me pre-homeless?"

All she could do was boggle at him. "Pre-homeless?"

"She caught me tossing half a burger in the trash. I'd already eaten a whole one. I was stuffed. Couldn't eat any more. She said I'd end up in the gutter, and that I belonged there, with the other sewage."

Sewage. Lydia had almost forgotten her mother's favored slur. "Oh, god."

"At the market, I heard her call Addison McGee a whore for getting that bluebird tattoo on her wrist. She called the Darling Songbirds country trash who didn't deserve their gold records. I saw her throw a slice of pumpkin bread at Josie in the bakery once because she thought it was too sweet. Your mom was a terrible person, and she was wrong about everything."

Lydia saw literal stars behind her eyelids, little explosions of light. "She was like that to everyone?"

Hawk nodded. "You never saw it because you tried not to be around her."

It was true. Once she got old enough to have friends with cars, Lydia tried to spend as little time as possible at home. "Oh. Oh, my."

He reached out and brushed a tendril of hair away from her eyes. "She was wrong about all of it."

"All of it," Lydia echoed. Something bright bloomed in her chest, an airy feeling of wonder. "All of it?"

"Yep." He took a breath. "That's really why you broke up with me back then?"

She nodded, her heart lodged in her throat.

"I thought it was because I was so bad at—" he opened his hands and gestured around the inside of the truck "—in here."

"Oh!" Heat washed over her. "No, you weren't that bad at all!"

He looked startled and then barked a laugh. "Thanks a lot."

"Come on, it was our first time." Lydia rested her hand on his wrist, and the words hung crystalline—almost visible—in front of them. *Our first time.*

Then he said them. "Our first time."

Lydia couldn't breathe. Hope was a bubble that would burst any second and—

He twined his fingers with hers. "Let's hope we get it right the second time."

"Hawk."

"And the twentieth."

"*Hawk.*"

"And the three-thousandth. You know what, Lydia St. Clair?"

"What?"

"I've been waiting to kiss you again for the last fifteen years. And I just don't think I can wait anymore."

With that, Hawk leaned forward and gathered her to him. His arms were around her, and somehow she was sitting on his very wet lap, her arms around his neck. His kiss was electric, sending shocks through her system while at the same time something sweet as honey poured through her veins.

"You know what?" he said against her mouth.

All she could say was "Mmm?" Her fingers kneaded the wet fabric at his chest. Surely he needed to go home and dry off. Could she help him with that?

"I've been in love with you since high school."

Lydia jolted backward, falling with a thump onto the seat next to him. "What?"

"I loved Erin, too. You know I did. You saw that. But she never, ever fit the Lydia spot in my heart. Only you do. Only you *could*. I can't believe I didn't know that until now."

"Ohhhh…" murmured Lydia. Happiness threatened to engulf her, washing her right out of the truck, so she kissed him again to see if the magic spell would wear off.

It didn't.

~

The next night—Christmas—the town was silent. The power had been out since eight that morning. The only place in town with a generator was the saloon, and as he and Lydia had walked that direction from his house, it shone like a miracle through the cold night. The rain had finally stopped, but the air was bitter cold. As they passed the café windows, they could see people eating in candlelight. Molly had obviously fired up the propane stovetop, and Hawk knew even without going inside that she'd have the Victrola playing music for the diners. Power outages were a pain in the ass. They were also beautiful in Darling Bay.

Inside the saloon, white lights twinkled from every corner. At least six people wore reindeer antlers and the air smelled of mulled spices, beer, and cinnamon. Over the laughter, "Adeste Fideles" was barely audible from the jukebox.

"I'll get us a drink." He dropped a kiss on Lydia's lips. She smiled up at him and simply said, "Okay."

His chest thumped.

She was here.

With him.

He wasn't going to let her go this time.

"Two Boonts, please," he said to Dixie.

"On another date with Lydia? On Christmas and everything? Looks serious, buddy," she teased.

But Hawk wasn't laughing. "It is serious." He never thought he'd get married again after Erin died. Now, after spending the night with Lydia wrapped in his arms, he knew that he'd walk down a million aisles if it meant she was at the end of each one. "I'm going to marry that woman."

Dixie choked. "Does she know that?"

"Not yet. But I think she has a suspicion." Maybe it was the fact that he'd asked Lydia what ring size she wore in the middle of the night.

This could just be the great sex talking, Lydia had laughed.

Yep. And more. And then Hawk had spent some quality time expanding upon the "more."

Now Dixie slid the beers across the bar to him. He offered her a twenty, and she shook her head. "No, way. We heard what you and Crystal and James and Josie did, setting up the memorial like that yesterday morning. The bowling alley looked amazing, and Earl would have been proud. Drinks on us tonight."

It *had* been a good memorial. A great one, even. Addison McGee's aunts had sung "How Great Thou Art" in four-part harmony (while Addison canoodled with Dylan, something Hawk was relieved to see), and when Cornie played "Amazing Grace" on the bagpipes, there hadn't been a dry eye in the alley. Then the whole town had stood around toasting Earl with cheap beer and the best barbecue wings in the whole world. Lydia had leaned against him at the end of the night, and nothing had ever felt better than putting his arm around her.

And at the end of the memorial, Crystal had gotten up on the shoe counter. Tipsily, she'd held up her arms. "I'm gonna read Earl's letter now! The last one! He's picked our next town Santa, and I get to tell you who it is!" With great ceremony and a bit of a wobble, she ripped open an envelope.

"Dear Darling Bay," she read. "If you're hearing Crystal read this, she's probably a little bit drunk and has taken her shoes off. Hey!" Crystal looked down in wonder at her shoe-less feet. Then she continued, "Santa never dies, so I've got to hand over my suit that I've loved wearing so much over the years. A great many men have asked me who would succeed me—" Hawk wondered exactly which men those were "—but there's only one in town who's fit to wear the red and white suit. Hawk Stokell is that man."

He heard Lydia giggle next to him.

"Hey, *what?*"

Crystal went on, "Because Hawk, you're the only six foot three guy in town who also weighs two hundred pounds. That suit has to fit just right. It ain't about your moral standing, though you're not too shabby at morality and at standing. Hawk, do me proud. Grow a beard. And kiss Lydia St. Clair while you're at it." Crystal peered over the paper. "That's him, Earl saying that! Not me!"

But Hawk had been so pleased by the direction to kiss Lydia he'd barely minded the Santa thing.

Until now, on Christmas Day, in the saloon.

"Where's your suit?" Addison asked. She was holding Dylan's hand and laughing up into his eyes.

"Yo, can I sit on your lap?" That one was from fire captain Tox Ellis.

"My chimney's dirty—if you clean it on your way down, I'll leave extra cookies next year," said Josie. "I left some out for you last night, but this guy stole them all." She nudged the San Francisco guy named James who looked delighted to be called a cookie thief.

But all he cared about was Lydia. He ignored the riffraff and carried her beer to her. "Well, I guess you're in love with a fantasy man."

She grinned. Damn, the woman was beautiful. Did her eyes ever tire of sparkling like that? "I guess I am," she said.

"I'm going to go put on the suit."

"You need help with that?"

"I do not." He took a sip of his beer and coughed on the foam. If she tried to help, he'd never get out of the bar's back room. "Be right back."

The suit was scratchy and heated up like a nuclear reactor as soon as he put it on. Hawk actually weighed closer to two-ten, and the belt strained a little. Well, that was to be expected with Santa, right? Earl had never had to use the fake white beard, having a real one of his own, but Hawk attached the one in the box around his ears.

He walked into the bar.

A roar went up. All eyes were on him and they were obviously waiting for him to *do* something.

For a moment, he didn't know what that was. He'd had a surfer period in his early twenties—should he flash a hang-loose? A peace sign?

Then it came to him. "Ho, ho, ho," he said feebly.

But they loved it. The crowd cheered again. His face itched like he'd woken up covered in poison oak.

It didn't matter, though. There, sandwiched between Norma on a barstool and the squat Christmas tree, was Lydia.

She wore a red dress that he only now realized matched his suit almost perfectly. High black heels. No makeup except lip gloss.

She was also wearing her heart on her sleeve, love shining in her eyes.

He had never seen anything prettier in his whole life.

He held up his arms. "I have one announcement before I let y'all sit on my lap and stuff dollar bills in my beard."

The bar quieted.

His heart sputtered and steamed like water on molten iron. For a brief second, he was scared enough to run out into the cold.

Then Lydia smiled at him again, and he felt braver than he'd ever felt before. He crossed the room and stood in front of her.

Then he knelt.

He heard an ominous ripping noise from the back of the suit but ignored it. "Lydia St. Clair, would you consider being Mrs. Claus someday? I mean, when it's reasonable, and we've been dating long enough for it not to be shock-ing, and—"

She cut him off by sitting on his knee and kissing him firmly on the mouth.

"Yes," she said, picking a white beard fuzzball off her lip.

A cheer rose, and when Hawk was done kissing the fuzz completely off Lydia's mouth, Norma's voice floated over their heads. *"Y'all! It's a goldarn white Christmas!"*

The crowd stampeded outside and into the silent street, carrying Hawk and Lydia along with them.

They stood together in joy, as the flakes fell from above, twisting and floating downward, sticking immediately to eyelashes and wondering fingers. Lydia tucked herself under Hawk's arm, and for the first time in years, he felt like his heart was all in one piece.

"I just have one condition on that Santa thing," she said into his ear.

"Anything," he promised, meaning it.

She tugged down his itchy beard and ran her fingers along his jaw. "Grow a real one for me."

"Done."

"And keep me on the naughty list, okay?"

Hawk laughed up into the white sky. Being Santa was, without a doubt, the best job he'd ever had.

ABOUT RACHAEL HERRON

Did you enjoy this story by Rachael Herron?
She'd love to hear from you!
https://www.facebook.com/Rachael.Herron.Author
http://twitter.com/rachaelherron
http://rachaelherron.com/blog
http://patreon.com/rachael

Rachael Herron is the bestselling author of the novels The Ones Who Matter Most, Splinters of Light and Pack Up the Moon (all from Penguin), the five-book Cypress Hollow series, and the memoir, A Life in Stitches. She received her MFA in writing from Mills College, Oakland. She teaches writing extension workshops at both UC Berkeley and Stanford and is a New Zealand citizen as well as an American. You can find her at RachaelHerron.com.

. . .

Need more Darling Bay in your life! Check out this free full-length novel! Keep reading for a preview of *The Darling Songbirds*!

A PREVIEW OF THE DARLING SONGBIRDS

The saloon had always looked old-fashioned, but now it resembled a set in a ghost town. The boards creaked under Adele Darling's feet as if they hadn't been stepped on since women wore hoop skirts. Cobwebs on the porch slung themselves from top beams to bottom ones, and an old wagon wheel leaned against a hitching post in front. It was as if the sidewalk had been poured right around the post, and her Toyota hybrid looked completely wrong parked next to it. It should have been a horse.

The problem was that Adele wasn't in an old western, or a ghost town. Darling Bay was the sleepy gold-rush town her great-grandfather had given his name to.

The town she'd left for good a long time ago.

There was a hand-drawn sign that said: *Hours – 11 AM– 2 AM.* She glanced at her cell phone. Almost noon, and the doors were locked. Awesome.

She knocked on the wood next to the iron screen door.

"That won't do you no good."

Adele spun. "Sorry?"

The exceedingly short woman standing on the step below her wore a long, oversized blue dress that hung on her like a sack. Somewhere in her mid-sixties, she had a well-creased face, like a crumpled envelope. A dozen or more necklaces dangled around her neck, crystals and quartz and what looked like actual feathers, on tarnished silver chains. Her short grey hair stuck up in spikes as if she'd just run her hands over it roughly, but her smile was wide. "He ain't here yet."

Adele wasn't sure who *he* was. "Okay . . ."

"But if you reach up above the door," the woman pointed, "yeah, right there. You're a tall one, ain't you? Grab that key for us, will you?"

It wasn't that Adele was tall at five foot five. It was more like the woman was eye level to her elbow. "Got it." Now that the key was in her hand, Adele had no idea what to do with it. It wasn't like she would just unlock the bar's front door. Would she?

She didn't have to make the decision. In a move so quick it surprised her, the woman snatched the key from her palm and unlocked the iron security door, swinging it wide open and barreling through the wooden half-door as if she owned the place, which Adele knew for a fact she didn't.

"Sometimes I gotta open up for him, you know?" The woman moved to the right and snapped on two light switches, and then headed for the bar. She was a low, fast-moving bowling ball in blue. "It's usually harder 'cause it's tough for me to reach that key. It's not like I mess with the till or nothin', I just help him out where I can."

Adele trailed behind the woman. This wasn't the situation she had imagined herself in when she'd awoken this morning. All she'd known four hours ago in her San Francisco hotel was that she had a long drive up the coast. When she got to Darling Bay, she figured she would plan her next move.

So she'd gotten in her rental car and headed north. Highway One wound through the redwoods, darting out to the rocky coast and back inland again. She'd stopped once to stretch her legs, and had stood cliff-side watching elephant seals slap themselves up and down the coarse sand. It took a bit more than three hours to get to Darling Bay, a long-enough drive to make her feel as far from Nashville as she'd ever felt.

She used to be used to this feeling. This used to be home.

And now she had exactly no idea what that meant.

"You want a drink, dearie?"

Adele blinked. "I'm sorry . . . Who are you?"

"Well, I suppose I could ask you the same thing."

That was fair. "I'm Adele Darling."

"Oh, my *God*. You *are*."

Crap. Adele should have just said her first name. What was she thinking? Nowhere else would her last name have raised more than a vaguely puzzled eyebrow. *Sounds familiar . . . can't place it.* But not here.

The woman clutched at her pile of necklaces. "They didn't tell me that."

"Who?" Adele was feeling more confused by the second. "I don't think anyone knew I was coming."

"But they usually tell me everything." She held up a

chain that had a pink piece of stone at the end and peered at it closely.

"Your necklaces tell you these things?" Adele kept her voice soft. Maybe it was better not to startle her.

The woman stared at Adele as if she were crazy. "Not my necklaces. My *dreams*."

"Ah."

"Of course, it's not like they're always right. Sometimes they tell me a storm is coming when all that's going to happen is I forget to take the kettle off the stove. Same thing." She waved her arms above her head. "Clouds of steam. Just in my kitchen. You see?"

Adele nodded carefully.

"Where are the other two?" The woman peered behind Adele as if she were somehow hiding her sisters.

"Not with me." Nothing could be truer. "I didn't get your name." Adele held out her hand.

The woman's shake was firm. "Norma."

"And you're the bartender?"

Norma laughed heartily, but she spread her palms on the top of the bar as if to negate her next statement. "Oh no, not me. You're a funny one. I'm just a drinker, from a long line of the same. Speaking of which, what can I make you?"

Not the bartender, then, but not *not* the bartender. "How about a Coke?"

"With rum? And can I read your tarot cards?" Norma asked hopefully.

"I'm good on both, thanks." It was a bit early to start pounding liquor. "So if you're not the bartender, and the saloon was supposed to open at eleven . . ."

"Oh, he'll be here."

"Who will?" This was beginning to feel like a game of Who's On First.

"Nate."

"Nate?"

"You don't know him?"

"I haven't been here in a while," Adele said. If a while meant eleven years. She'd been far away from Darling Bay, sometimes as far as a person could get. "*When* do you think he'll be here?"

Norma frowned and held one of her necklaces, looking upward as if the answer hung in the cobwebbed rafters. "Soon." Then she filled a glass with Coke and slid it towards Adele. "Here you go. Now, tell me everything. How're your sisters? You know, my dad – may he rest in peace – died before y'all got famous, but I always think he would have loved you. When *your* dad died, I asked my dad to bring him into heaven with a big ol' hug. Felt so bad for you young gals. Are you getting the band back together? You know we talk about you all the time. And those magazines, they stopped printing those stories about y'all, and that's a good thing, but we never believed a word they said anyway. How's the little one? Lana?"

The back of Adele's throat itched. "Fine." She had no idea how Lana was since she never answered Adele's phone calls. The ache of it was dull and familiar. "Do you mind if I have a look around? While I wait for Nate?"

"Sure, sure." Norma bobbed up and down behind the bar, spinning into action. Tomato juice, sliced celery, vodka. "A Bloody Mary doesn't just appear out of nowhere. Gotta work at it." She frowned and looked upward again.

"Unless you stare into the mirror, you know? And say those words? I'm not gonna do *that*. Okay. There." She added a dash of Tabasco. "Mine isn't as good as Nate's, but I'm getting there. Just gotta keep working on it."

Adele wandered towards the rear of the saloon. It was just as she remembered it, dark and dusty, smelling of splintered wood and spilled beer. The old jukebox glowed neon blue and green in the far right corner. Next to it was a skinny ATM that had been added since she was last here. To the left of that ran the long bar all the way to the back wall. How many buckets of ice had Adele hauled out of the old storeroom? The girls had loved being there in the saloon, still under-age, helping Uncle Hugh with stocking and refilling in the afternoons. They'd begged to be allowed to stay as late as they could, listening to the music, not leaving until Sheriff Tate came in after his shift and raised his eyebrows at the little girls doing their homework in the far left corner on the big, scarred wooden table.

The table was still there. Adele touched the top of it, feeling the ridges with her fingertips. People still carved their initials into it, using penknives and ballpoint pens. They didn't cut deeply (out of respect, perhaps – surely they would have dug more deeply into a tree) and the well-worn initials looped over each other, years and years of couples who had loved and lost and loved again. When Adele and her sisters had done their math homework here, they'd had to make sure their notepads were under their papers, or their pencils would stab through into the table's scars.

Somewhere on the table were their initials, too. All three of them, *AD + MD + LD. Adele and Molly and Lana.*

Hidden now somewhere, buried by the map of other letters.

Adele realized she was humming and closed her throat. She heard the refrain of "You'll Never Leave" in her mind. Then she wandered back towards the front door. To the right was the stage. Just a couple of feet higher than the floor, it was made of the same old wood and, if she remembered right, just as rickety. Impulsively, she jumped up onto it, stretching her arms wide. A light snapped on above her head, and she grinned in delight. Even when they were kids, Uncle Hugh had kept that motion-activated light there, and they'd loved the way it had shone down on them like a spotlight.

"Sing us a song!" called Norma from the other side of the saloon.

Oh, hell, no. Adele swallowed her grin and raised a hand. "Maybe later." Or maybe never.

The old pool table stood in the same spot it always had. Adele could imagine a tsunami sweeping in and taking out the Golden Spike, carrying away the saloon and the café and the old hotel – the whole town of Darling Bay itself – but that pool table, as heavy as sin and older than Eve's apple, would stay right there, right where it had always been meant to sit. At some point over the years, the felt playing top had been repaired. Chalks, the old square kind, were lined up on the rail, and a half-dozen cue sticks leaned drunkenly against the short inner wall.

Adele could almost hear the crack of the balls. Molly had been their ringer, always willing to bat her eyes innocently at whatever guy thought it would be fun to show off his pool prowess to teenage girls. Molly would run the table, stick the guy's money in her pocket, and then ask Uncle Hugh for a round of root beer floats for her and her sisters.

Molly. She wanted Molly here.

She pulled out her cell phone. *Remember the root beer floats?*

Holding her phone in her hand in case the text actually managed to soar out to the cruise ship somewhere on the ocean, Adele used her other hand to lift up the bench seat in the front window alcove. There they were, all the board games they'd spent so much time with. She'd be willing to bet that the Monopoly set was still missing all the Get Out of Jail Free cards. (Sheriff Tate had gotten his feelings hurt one night when he'd been on a particularly expensive Monopoly losing streak.) And the Sorry! game . . . She pulled it out and lifted the lid. Yep, there they were. Each piece had little teeth marks at the top, marching all the way around. The blue piece was missing the round knobby top altogether.

While Adele raced around the board, passing her sisters with a cheery "Sorry!" Lana would get so mad she'd chew the pieces, leaving her tooth marks behind, or in the case of the blue one, biting the top right off.

Adele glanced left. Norma was looking into her Bloody Mary as if it were telling a fortune, so Adele quietly slipped the headless blue piece into her jeans pocket. From the layers of dust inside the bench seat, no one would miss the piece anytime soon.

She looked out the side alcove window. Across the middle parking lot stood the old café. Funny, she'd assumed it would still be open, that Hugh's employees would still be running it. But it was shuttered and dark, an unbearable sense of loneliness coming from the ripped awning. The old caboose that had been a coffee stand rusted in front, near the sidewalk. She looked right, up to the slight rise behind the saloon and café. That was the hotel, the third old building that she'd called home every summer of her youth. It was where she would sleep tonight. She yearned for that, for this already-long day to speed up until she could just lie down, close her eyes, and breathe in the ocean-scented air.

The phone – the real one that hung on the bar's back wall – jangled. Adele jumped. Norma grabbed it without hesitation. "Golden Spike, this is Norma!"

There was a pause. "Yeah." She grinned. "Right again. You bet. I'll keep 'er running, boss. Yeah. Okay. And hey? I forgot to tell you I need a raise." She slammed the phone down with a hoot of laughter. "That was him!" She looked at Adele as if suddenly surprised to see her. "Oh! I should have told him you were here."

"No, that's okay. I'll see him when he gets here."

"So I guess *you're* the boss around here now." Norma was obviously startled by the thought, her grey eyebrows shooting higher. "Of course you are. Oooh." Her drink wrapped tightly in her hand, she leaned forward from her bar stool. "You should tell him to hire me. I wouldn't drink all the booze, I *swear* I wouldn't." But there was a twinkle behind her expression that said the opposite was true, and that they both knew it.

Nate shouldn't have answered his cell phone that morning, but he was a sucker for a blonde. Especially if the blonde happened to be ninety-one and living on the boat he'd sold her five months earlier. Ruthann Suthers had asked, "Does it matter, dear, if my extension cord in the kitchen smokes a little?" Nate thought of the electrical fire at the hotel, and told her to call 911. She said, "I already did. They said it was okay, but they shut off my power." Nate had sighed and spent the next two hours crawling around the baseboards in the boat's mess. He'd installed three new surge protectors, and he'd tested each outlet. By the time he'd finished, he'd bruised a knuckle and ripped his favorite Merle Haggard T-shirt.

And he was late.

At least Norma had been at the bar to open up. Unless a wandering tourist or two showed up, she'd probably be the only customer until three, anyway.

He parked his truck in front of the post office. Getting

out, he pulled his Charlie's Feed and Seed ball cap on backward. What he really needed was another shower. Maybe he could bribe Norma with a couple more drinks off her tab to stay a little longer while he cleaned up. He took the two shallow steps up off street level with one long jump.

Inside the saloon it was dim compared to the bright morning sunlight. Norma grinned at him from her regular bar stool. "Boss!"

"You keeping out the riffraff?" Too late, he noticed that someone else *was* in the saloon, way over by the bench full of board games. "Whoops." Not even a tourist – a pretty tourist, at that – wanted to be called riffraff.

"Nah, they're getting in. And hey, guess who it is."

He looked again. The woman was standing straighter now, pretending not to hear them. She kept her eyes out the side alcove window as if there was something more than just the old, closed Golden Spike Café across the parking lot to look at. And she wasn't just pretty. From this angle, she was a sight closer to beautiful. God, who did she remind him of? She must have driven up from the city or something. Some model, waiting for her photographer to shoot her on the beach. He'd seen it plenty of times before, pretty girls thinking it would be good to get shots of themselves in the water, or leaning against the high cliffs down at Fenton's Cove, not realizing that the fog bank usually made it not only a shoot in bad light, but also a shoot where they'd freeze their dang nipples off. If they stayed till October, maybe. That's when the sun came out around here, after the summer tourists had given up all hope and left. But this woman, with her honeyed hair and that perfect long nose, those lips that were quirking into something that looked like it was close to a smile, she'd be shivering in her two-piece soon enough.

"Howdy," he said politely. If his ball cap had been forward-facing, he would have touched the brim, but as it was he left his arms at his sides.

She turned to face him, and in that motion his heart dropped to the old floorboards and went right through, straight down to the dust and packed earth below, not stopping until it hit the world's molten core.

Adele Darling. Out of freaking *nowhere.*

Keep Reading! Go here:
http://rachaelherron.com/ds1_a
And get the rest of the book for free!